Chasing The Wind

by

Sandra Seaton Michel

A Copper Country Mystery

Feather Pen Publishing

Cover Design: Lydia Michel Wong

The author gratefully acknowledges the editorial and publishing guidance of David Michel.

Order online at amazon.com

Prologue
July 10,1870
Red Jacket, Michigan

Frustrated and angry, Alexander impatiently yanked the reins as he turned the buggy onto the long, curving driveway. Halfway up the driveway, he pulled the horse to a stop and sat looking at his home. Bathed in light from an early moon, the huge, white house looked particularly lovely with the yellow glow from the first floor windows beckoning bright and welcoming in the summer night.

Susannah would be inside, waiting for him, wondering why he was so late, but determined not to become upset, not to nag him about the long hours he worked, not to spoil the excitement and anticipation of tomorrow. He wondered how he could face her. And what could he possibly tell her?

Slowly he climbed down from the buggy and began to lead the horse forward. He frowned, puzzled by an odd, flickering light in dining room window, then whirled as someone charged out of the darkness. Caught off guard he was slammed to the ground.

Looming over him, shaking with rage, was Anasta Thropyleus.

"Now, Mr. Thief, I got you! From my brother's family you took all. Now, you look, I take all from you. I fire you house and you I kill." The stocky, work-toughened miner reached for the pistol stuck in his belt.

Alexander rolled sideways, scrambled to his feet and lunged forward grabbing Anasta's wrist. The two men struggled for the gun. Grunting and shoving, staggering backward and forward, the stronger miner gradually turned the gun towards Alexander's stomach. Fear strengthening the slightly built, wiry accountant, Alexander forced the gun back towards Anasta as it went off.

Anasta Thropyleus groaned and fell to the ground. Stunned, Alexander stared at the blood spreading across his assailant's chest.

He turned towards the house. Flames and smoke burst from the dining room windows.

"Susannah! Susannah!" he yelled, running to the house. A window slammed open on the second floor. Smoke billowed out. Susannah leaned out, coughing and gasping, with their child in her arms.

"Susannah! I'm here. Below you. Drop Catherine, I'll catch her. Then you jump too. I will catch you."

Susannah dropped Catherine. Alexander braced himself to catch his five-year-old daughter. Even so, he was knocked to the ground. Barely noticing she was unconscious, he leaped up to catch his wife. She was not at the window.

"Susannah! Susannah. Susannah!" Only smoke appeared at the window. Alexander ran to the front door and pulled it open. Heat blasted him backward. The front stairs were ablaze. He turned and ran to the back of the house. It was worse there. Alexander ran to the barn and grabbed a ladder.

Lungs aching from smoke and exertion, he ran to the front of the house and set the ladder up at the bedroom window. Rapidly he climbed the rungs. Smoke engulfed him as he climbed through the window. He did not have to search, Susannah lay by the window. Coughing, choking, he picked her up and carried her down the ladder.

Gently, he laid his wife on the lawn. Desperately, he searched for a heartbeat, a breath, a little movement, something, anything. Nothing. Stunned, he touched her auburn hair, her lovely face. Carefully, he straightened her dress. The long skirt did not quite cover the heavy, leather boot she wore on her clubfoot. He knelt, looking at the boot, wondering if she had been downstairs when the fire began. Yes, he thought, first Susannah would go to the kitchen to see what was causing the smoke. But if Anasta Thropyleus started it with kerosene the kitchen would have been blazing and Susannah would run to save Catherine. But she could not run. With her club foot she couldn't even climb the stairs fast enough to save both Catherine and herself.

Catherine coughed and gagged. Her eyes were open now, staring, transfixed at the burning house.

Alexander turned to her, picked her up and carried her to the buggy.

Chapter 1
July 17, 1870
Grand Falls, Illinois

Sitting quietly on the bench, back straight, hands folded on her lap, legs swinging gently back and forth, Catherine waited in the cool, dark hall. Her father was in the room across the hall. A room with books, rows and rows of books, lining the walls, and a big desk, polished and gleaming like a dining room table.

The door opened and her father came out of the room. He looked tired and travel worn, not at all like his normal, dapper self. Holding out his hand he said, "Come Catherine." She jumped down from the bench and moved eagerly to his side, taking his hand. Together the slightly built dark haired man and the sturdy, auburn haired child entered the study.

"Now Catherine," her father spoke in the 'isn't this wonderful voice' that every child knows means that what is about happen will not be wonderful at all. "This is Reverend and Mrs. Ogilve. They are going to look after you for a time. Isn't that fine? You will live right here with them in this lovely town." Gently, he pulled his hand from hers and urged her towards the Ogilves.

Solemnly, Catherine looked at them. She knew she could not go home; her father had explained that. Explained that her mother was dead, their house burned down, and there was no one to look after her. She knew that, but she did not understand it.

"Why don't we build a new house and have Marta and Elsie look after me?" she kept asking. Her father would shake his head and say, "No. No, that is just not possible."

"Catherine, have you nothing to say?" her father asked as she stood rooted in silence. She shook her head, pressing against his leg.

Reverend Ogilve smiled. "I think I would be frightened, too, if I were a child. After all, you've not met us before. I expect we look quite strange and frightening to you. However, Catherine, I do believe you will find we are not too difficult to get along with." His deep resonant voice and smiling brown eyes, brimming with curiosity and compassion, reached out to the frightened child and helped her begin to relax. A half smile appeared briefly. He really did not look frightening.

Mrs. Ogilve, however, was a bit frightening. She was neat and precise in appearance and movement and spoke in a soft, firm voice.

"Catherine, your father has asked us to take care of you for awhile. Reverend Ogilve and I have agreed to do so." She paused, watching the frightened child shrink against her father's leg. "You are quite confused, I'm sure. Your father tells us you are five years old and that it has only been a week since your mother died."

Catherine looked up at her father and pleaded, "I want to stay with you, Daddy. Why can't I stay with you? Please, Daddy!"

"Catherine," he spoke with a weary sadness, "I've told you and told you, it cannot be. I'll be traveling all of the time. It is no proper life for a child. You need looking after and you begin school in a few weeks. You must understand."

She did not understand the reasons but she did understand she was helpless to change the outcome. When Mrs. Ogilve said, "Come along, Catherine. I will show you to your room." Catherine followed her.

They crossed the cool, dark hall and climbed the front stairs to the second floor. Light from windows at each end of the upstairs hall fell on the worn hall rug and the hot, humid summer heat felt oppressive compared to the cooler downstairs.

Mrs. Ogilve and Catherine entered the room at the top of the stairs on the left. "This will be your room, Catherine. It was our son's, but he is grown now and has a home of his own. Reverend Ogilve and I have the room in the front on the right. Across the hall from our room is the guest bedroom. The room across from yours is my sewing room."

Catherine looked around the large room. There was a narrow bed against the far wall, covered with a blue, white, and yellow quilt. Next to the bed was a bookcase. A large dresser with a built-in mirror was the only other furniture in the room. The wood floor was bare except for a small rag rug by the bed. Two large windows were set in the wall opposite the door.

Slowly Catherine walked to a window and looked out. There was a huge elm just outside of the window, its branches almost within reach and she could hear children playing nearby.

When Catherine turned back to the room Mrs. Ogilve was gone and her father was carrying in her valise. He unpacked her clothes and placed them in the bureau drawers. As he unpacked, he told her what a grand time she would have in Grand Falls and how he knew she would soon love the Ogilves. And she must be a good girl and obey them as if they were her parents. And please not to look so sad, for he would be back to visit before she noticed he was gone - and besides, school would be starting in a few weeks and wouldn't that be exciting!

Catherine listened but did not respond. She was very tired. The week of traveling, getting up at odd hours, riding boats and trains and never staying in the same place two days in a row, had worn her out. Now, the draining summer heat seemed to steal what strength she had left.

The unpacking finished, they went downstairs for a light supper. The Ogilves and her father talked while Catherine sat drooping, barely eating. When the meal was over, as her father carried her to bed, she fell asleep in his arms. Gently, he removed her clothes, slipped her into her nightgown, placed her on the bed, and pulled the sheet over her.

He sat on the edge of the bed watching her sleep, then bent to kiss her. Tears welling in his eyes overflowed and fell on her cheek. Softly he brushed them away, blessing his child as he did so.

The next morning Catherine walked into the kitchen as the Ogilves were about to sit down to breakfast.

"Good morning, Catherine," Reverend Ogilve greeted her pleasantly. "Do come and sit down."

Eyes down, Catherine walked across the worn wood floor and slipped onto a chair. Placed on the crisp, white tablecloth were plates of bread, jam, sliced fresh peaches, brown sugar, and a pitcher of thick cream. Carefully she spread her napkin on her lap. It was embroidered around the edges with red and yellow flowers and green leaves.

Adding her own, "Good Morning, Catherine," Mrs. Ogilve placed a large bowl of porridge at each place and sat down. Reverend

Ogilve gave the blessing. "We thank you Lord for this beautiful day and for the good food you have provided to sustain our bodies. Guide us and Catherine as we commence to live together for these next months. Watch over Catherine's father and bring him safely back to us in the spring. These things we ask in Jesus' name. Amen."

Catherine stared at her porridge wondering if she had to eat it all. She sprinkled on brown sugar, carefully poured on cream, and, sighing, picked up her spoon.

The Ogilves talked of matters foreign to Catherine as they ate. They did not try to include her, sensing it was better to let her be for the moment. Finished eating, Reverend Ogilve thanked his wife for an excellent breakfast and excused himself.

Mrs. Ogilve remained at the table drinking a second cup of tea, waiting for Catherine to finish eating. She realized the child was struggling to finish.

"Eat only as much as you want, Catherine. When you feel full, stop. No doubt, I gave you too large a portion. I've forgotten just how much, or how little, a five-year-old eats."

Catherine sighed and laid down her spoon but she did not look up. She seemed fascinated with the edge of her cereal bowl. Mrs. Ogilve waited and finally Catherine looked up. Mrs. Ogilve began speaking again.

"Catherine, you were very sleepy last night so I am not sure what you understood of our conversation with your father." She paused but there was no response. "Do you understand that you are to live with us for the time being?"

Catherine nodded.

"That being understood," Mrs. Ogilve continued, "I think we shall get along best if you clearly understand our household rules. I'm sure your mother also had rules and no doubt you will find many of our rules are the same.

"There is to be no running or shouting in the house. No running up the stairs, no sliding down the banister. You may play in your room or in the yard. You may not play in the office, the parlor, or the dining room. You may sit in the parlor to read or when we have company. Most particularly, you are not to touch the piano in the parlor. A piano is not a toy.

"We eat breakfast at eight, dinner at twelve, and supper at six. You are expected to be on time. We do not wait. If you miss a meal you will do without. Also, you are to bush your hair and wash your hands and face before each meal."

Catherine was listening carefully. She did understand not running or shouting in the house and washing before meals because her mother expected the same behavior. But how was she to tell when it was eight or twelve or six? Marta had always dressed her, brushed her hair and sent her to breakfast. Her mother told her when it was time for dinner and supper.

"You will be expected to keep your bedroom neat at all times and to make your bed before you come to breakfast. Also, you will help me in the kitchen. I realize there is not a lot you can do at your age but you can fetch things and help set and clear the table.

"Those are the basic rules. Do you have questions about any of them?"

Glancing at Mrs. Ogilve and then looking away, Catherine replied softly, "I don't know how to make my bed and I can't tell time."

"Not tell time or know how to make your bed," Mrs. Ogilve could not hide the astonishment from her voice. "Well, in that case, we must teach you. However, until you learn to read a clock, I will call you at mealtimes. As for making a bed, you can begin learning to do that this morning."

Mrs. Ogilve looked at the woebegone child sitting at the kitchen table. Her long auburn curls had not been brushed, her hair ribbon was tied in a knot, her cotton dress was not buttoned properly.

"I don't know how to set the table, either." Catherine spoke a bit louder this time.

"Did you not help your mother in the kitchen when she was cooking your meals?"

"No. Elsie cooked the meals."

"Was Elsie your sister?"

"Elsie was the cook!" Catherine's tone implied that everyone knew that.

"Did Elsie make your bed too?"

"Marta made the beds."

"I see," said Mrs. Ogilve. "Well, in this house we do not have servants. We must do things for ourselves. Let us begin by clearing the table and doing the dishes. Then I will show you how to make your bed and brush your hair."

As they began to clear the table Harriet Ogilve wondered, why would a man with money enough to employ servants need us to care for his daughter? And how in the world did we let ourselves be talked into taking care of a child we know nothing about!

Chapter 2

And so the new life began. With a deep sadness and somewhat fearfully, Catherine began to adjust. She liked the Reverend Donald Taylor Ogilve. He made her smile.

Donald Ogilve loved children and was able to project it. He often had the largest Sunday School and Young Peoples Bible Fellowship of any church in Grand Falls. Other clergy wondered what special, outstanding program he offered that attracted young people. It was not the program, but rather that children felt his love and acceptance and sought its source.

Catherine was intimidated by Mrs. Ogilve whose graying hair stayed perfectly in its bun and whose clothes always looked freshly pressed as she moved briskly from task to task. And certainly she had a lot to do. Besides her regular household tasks of cooking, cleaning and sewing, she also preserved fruits and vegetables from her large garden. Her duties as the minister's wife included attending women's meetings, visiting the elderly and entertaining callers at the manse. She was also the church organist and choir director. Her one concession to human weakness was employing a laundress.

Cautiously, Catherine began to explore her new home. The top floor was a large attic filled with old furniture. The basement was cold and dark. The second floor, where she had her bedroom was bright and cheerful. She liked the second floor. Even Mrs. Ogilve's sewing room seemed a friendly place.

The first floor was quiet. Here Catherine felt she should walk and talk softly. On one side of the long entrance hall were the dining room and kitchen. Dinner was eaten in the dining room with its high ceiling, long, narrow windows and darkly gleaming table and buffet. Breakfast and supper were served in the kitchen.

Reverend Ogilve's study and the parlor were on the other side of the hall. The room that fascinated Catherine was the parlor. Set in the front of the house, it had two windows facing onto the porch and a large bay window at the corner of the house. It was furnished with heavy, dark walnut chairs and a sofa. A faded oriental rug covered the floor.

This was the room with the piano. The piano she was not to touch.

Positioned to catch the best light from the windows, its polished wood reflected years of loving care. It sparkled and beckoned to Catherine. When Mrs. Ogilve was outside working in the garden Catherine would go to the parlor and look at the piano. Each time she looked, she came a little closer.

Finally, came the day when the piano could no longer be resisted. She pulled out the piano bench, climbed up and pushed back the cover over the keys. Tentatively she touched middle C, pressing just hard enough to make a sound. Then, worrying that she had been heard she went to the bay window expecting to see Mrs. Ogilve hurrying towards the house. But Mrs. Ogilve was busy pulling weeds and did not even glance towards the window.

Catherine returned to the piano and began to play softly. Soon she forgot to be afraid, forgot everything except the piano.

Harriet Ogilve was surprised to hear piano music. Odd, she thought, it sounds as if it's coming from the front parlor. Harriet walked towards the window. Definitely, someone was playing simple tunes.

Curious, she continued to the front of the house, stripping off her gardening gloves as she climbed the steps and setting them on the porch railing.

Catherine heard footsteps on the porch. Heart pounding, she yanked her hands from the keyboard.

"Well, child, what is this?" Mrs. Ogilve asked as she entered the parlor. Catherine was amazed. Mrs. Ogilve did not sound angry. "You did not tell me you could play."

"My mother taught me," Catherine whispered.

"What a happy surprise." Mrs. Ogilve smiled at Catherine and sat next to her on the piano bench. "Now, let's see what you know. Please play something for me."

Looking up sideways at Mrs. Ogilve, Catherine hesitated. Mrs. Ogilve nodded encouragement. Finally, convinced she was not to be punished, Catherine concentrated on the piano and played all she could remember.

Then Mrs. Ogilve began to play. Catherine was surprised how happy she felt as Mrs. Ogilve played. If I close my eyes, she thought, I can pretend it is my mother playing.

Engrossed in the music, neither Catherine nor Mrs. Ogilve noticed the passing time nor did they hear Reverend Ogilve enter the house.

"What have we here?" he asked, seeing the two of them sitting at the piano. "Don't tell me Catherine likes music?"

"Indeed she does. Likes it and plays it. Plays it well, I might add," said Mrs. Ogilve, smiling at Catherine who was astonished at the complement and could not help but smile back. "She has much to learn, of course. We shall begin lessons tomorrow. I will find the time. Is that agreeable with you, Catherine?"

"Yes. Oh, please, yes," was Catherine's joyful response.

That evening, as the Ogilves prepared for bed, Harriet commented, "Is it not amazing, Donald, that Catherine did not know how to tell time, did not know her last name, but reads music and plays the piano quite well?"

Donald emptied the contents of his pockets and arranged them neatly on his dresser. "She does seem talented, my dear. Perhaps giving her lessons will make her feel more at home. She is such a quiet, sad little bit of a mouse."

"Little bit of a mouse!" protested Harriet. "She is hardly little, in fact, she is tall for her age and not a bit drab looking. But you are right about the sadness. I think today is the first time I've seen her truly smile.

"What worries me, Donald, is that we may be too old for the child. Did you know I forbade her to touch the piano? It would have been a terrible, terrible wrong if she had obeyed me."

"Ah, but she did not obey you. I wouldn't worry too much. It will work out, and Catherine will settle in." He laughed, "I think she has already. Did you hear her run up the stairs to wash up for supper? Just like William did when he was five."

"I suppose so. Still, I will feel better when Alexander Duncan returns for her in the spring."

The Ogilves lived in Grand Falls, Illinois. A small town with a population of 12,000 located 50 miles southwest of Chicago. The origin of the name was a mystery for the town was located alongside the wide, flat, Pontiac River with never a hint of rapids, much less falls, in sight. The area's rich soil and long, hot summers were excellent for crops, and the town's main business was providing supplies for farms and then shipping the farms' produce to Chicago.

When school started Catherine discovered that she did like it, just as her father said she would. Seeing what her father said come true helped but she was still confused and frightened about why he had left her. But he said she would like school and he said he would come for her again. If the one was true, and now she knew it was, then the other would also be true.

But as the weeks passed and she heard nothing from her father, Catherine became fearful again. She did not want to ask the Ogilves about her father, she wanted him to be hers alone, but his absence and silence overwhelmed her and she asked Mrs. Ogilve when would he come for her.

"I do not know your father's plans Catherine, other than he did say he would be back for you in the late spring or early summer."

After that, Catherine occasionally asked how much longer it was until spring but other than that did not talk about her family. It puzzled the Ogilves for it appeared that she had wiped away her past, but being reserved and private individuals themselves, they did not press her.

Catherine had not forgotten. She thought about her parents every day and often dreamed about them at night. Sometimes she and her mother sat side by side playing the piano. While they were playing, her mother would look at her and smile, and Catherine would feel warm and happy as they played beautiful music. It was always the same music. During the day, Catherine tried to remember how it went, but she could not. In some dreams, her mother, bathed in light, bright, shining sunlight, held her and rocked her.

There were bad dreams too. Dreams of black night and red flames and she was afraid. She ran and ran from the black night and the red flames, but the red flames ran faster. They reached out to grab her and the harder she ran the slower her legs moved and the flames came closer and closer. She would jerk awake with her heart pounding.

Catherine daydreamed, too. Daydreamed about her father returning. She would be his "Special Princess" again and they would play happy games. He would read bedtimes stories and tuck her into bed. Most of all, she liked to remember his laughter because when he laughed she laughed too, and he would give her a big hug as they laughed together.

Sometimes, when Catherine thought about her father, she worried he would not come back. She decided the best way to be sure he really returned was to be a very good girl.

She would obey the Ogilves, do well in school, and practice the piano every day. Especially the piano, because both of her parents had praised her piano playing.

Abigail Key was Catherine's first grade teacher. Miss Key loved children and teaching. When she saw the solemn-eyed redhead walk into her class she sensed the child's loneliness and isolation and reached out to help her. Soon, Catherine became her adoring shadow and when Miss Key gave her a good mark or word of praise Catherine glowed thinking how pleased her father was going to be when he returned.

The months passed slowly but school finally ended. Catherine's father had not returned, but Catherine knew he would arrive soon. Each morning, she jumped out of bed and ran to the guest bedroom to see if he had come while she was sleeping. Each day she played by the house to be there when he arrived. Even when other children went on picnics along the river Catherine stayed home to be there when her father returned.

In July, Rev. and Mrs. Ogilve traveled to Chicago for the marriage of their son, Peter, to Hulda Baumgarten. Catherine refused to go with them panicked her father would come while she was away and not be able to find her. She stayed with a neighbor while the Ogilves were in Chicago.

Harriet Ogilve did her best to persuade Catherine to go with them. She told her they would leave a note for her father on the door of the house and the neighbors would watch for Mr. Duncan. She told her Chicago was an exciting city and they all were to be guests in the Baumgarten's lovely mansion.

She did not tell Catherine she was disappointed that Peter was not the college professor he planned to be when he entered Oberlin College in 1862. An ardent abolitionist, Peter left Oberlin at the end of his first year to enlist in the Army of the Republic.

He fought throughout the war with only a few minor wounds and reached the rank of captain. The idealistic teacher evaporated on the battlefields. The young man who returned did not want to put in years of study before he could think of earning a decent income. He settled in Chicago seeking a position in the business world. Herman Baumgarten hired him, tutored him in the furniture business, and was delighted when Peter and his daughter, Hulda, made plans to marry.

Harriet and Donald were not ecstatic over the upcoming wedding because Hulda seemed a pampered snob. But, if Peter wanted to marry her they were wise enough to keep their opinions to themselves and go, smiling, to the wedding.

Catherine barely noticed there was a wedding. She thought only of her father's return as hot summer day after hot summer day, she waited.

When school began again Catherine stopped looking for her father. She tried to stop thinking about him. She tried not to feel lonely, and angry, and frightened. She struggled to push those feelings away and to believe he would come. Nothing else was possible. He would come. He had to come. Someday.

Chapter 3
Fifteen Years Later
June 5, 1885
Grand Falls, Illinois

"Catherine, come and see if I left anything at the back of the shelf in this closet," Harriet Ogilve's voice echoed through the empty rooms.

"I checked all of the closets a little while ago." Cate answered from across the hall as she finished washing the bedroom windows. "But I'll check again if you want me too."

"No. Once is quite enough. It is time for a cup of tea anyway. I hear the kettle steaming."

Cate finished the windows, collected her wash bucket and rags, and followed Mrs. Ogilve to the kitchen.

"It seems so strange you won't be living in this house." Cate said as she entered the kitchen. "I know the manse belongs to the church and the new minister and his family will live here but..."

"There are no buts about it, my dear," said Mrs. Ogilve as she set bread and jam on the table. "We always knew we'd leave this house when Donald retired."

Cate put away her bucket and rags, washed up, and joined Mrs. Ogilve at the kitchen table. The strong, black tea was poured and silence reigned as cream and sugar were added and the first heartening sips taken.

"It is good to sit down." Cate sighed and arched her stiffening shoulders. "I'm afraid I've become a spoiled lady of leisure at Oberlin."

"I very much doubt that! Not unless the college has gone downhill since our Peter attended," Harriet Ogilve stated emphatically and then smiled fondly at Cate. "You know, Catherine, Rev. Ogilve was proud of your academic accomplishments. He had so looked forward to attending your graduation."

Overcome with emotion, Harriet Ogilve stopped speaking. Learning to live without Donald was difficult and speaking about him extremely difficult. But live without him she must do and speaking about him, though still a struggle, she would do.

Cate reached across the table and took her hand as, with a slight tremble in her voice, Mrs. Ogilve continued. "When Rev. Ogilve had his first stroke, I debated sending you a telegram, but the doctor said it was not a serious one and it was so close to your exams that we did not want to distract you. The doctor expected that he would fully recover. It was not to be. His second stroke, just three weeks later, was fatal.

"When that happened, it was a comfort to know we had lasted long enough to see you through to your graduation."

"How did you manage it? I know you don't like to talk about financial matters and perhaps I shouldn't bring it up, but I have wondered. Oberlin costs $450 a year for tuition, books, room and board, and music fees!"

"It's true," Mrs. Ogilve agreed, "when you were a child we did not want you to worry about financial matters but you are an adult now and there is no reason you should not be told. Your education was paid for with the money your father gave us when he first brought you to us.

"Your father gave Rev. Ogilve one thousand dollars to be used for your care," Harriet continued. "It was such a large amount we assumed it was his life savings and that he would need it when he returned for you. When your father did not return at the end of the first year we feared something had happened to him, an accident or illness perhaps. Rev. Ogilve decided to invest the money and use it for your education or, if anything happened to us before you were grown, for your care."

"A thousand dollars," Cate repeated stunned. "That is such a large amount. Are there other things about my father that you haven't told me?"

"I'm not sure. I think we told you what little we knew years ago. But I did find something in the study that may belong to you. A leather case. As soon as I saw it I thought of your father. I know Rev. Ogilve did not have such a case. It is in the bookcase in the bottom cabinet on the left. Why don't you get it?"

Harriet smiled watching Catherine walk out of the kitchen. She had become the daughter she and Donald yearned for but never had. And what a wonderful daughter indeed. Harriet could not deny that it was satisfying to know they had a hand in raising this intelligent young woman who walked confidently, talked properly, dressed modestly, and had a smile for everyone. Nor could she deny it gave her great pleasure that Catherine was so attractive. She smiled to herself knowing that Catherine, who had been raised with the admonition that only inward beauty counted, would have been quite surprised that Mrs. Ogilve even noticed.

Cate returned with the leather case inscribed with the initials A. D. McL.

"Do you really think it was my father's?" she asked setting it on the table. "The initials are not correct."

"Yes, I noticed that too. But still, when I first saw the case I immediately thought of your father."

"Should we open it?" Cate asked, eager to see the contents.

"I am afraid it is locked," Mrs. Ogilve replied. "Perhaps we should take it to a locksmith."

Cate examined the case carefully. "I think I could pry the latches open with a screwdriver. And then we won't have to pay a locksmith," she added with a grin. Mrs. Ogilve agreed and after a few abortive attempts, Cate popped the latches and opened the case.

It was filled with envelopes and papers. Catherine picked up the top envelope. Inside were packs of bank notes, neatly tied together. Stunned she passed the envelope to Mrs. Ogilve. Next, in a soft leather bag was a silver picture frame holding a photograph of a family. The man stood behind a chair, a woman sat on the chair, a young child sat on the woman's lap. They were elegantly dressed and the photo was well composed but it was not the wealth or composition that caught the eye but, rather, the sense of joy shinning from the serious faces. Catherine handed it to Mrs. Ogilve.

"Why Catherine, that is you and your father," she exclaimed. "That is just as you looked when you came to us. This must be your mother with you. Yes, I can see a distinct resemblance to your adult self."

Eagerly Cate examined the photo. She had long forgotten what her parents looked like but trusted Mrs. Ogilves memory for herself and her father. As she looked at her family, she suddenly drew in her breath. Mrs.

Ogilve glance at her inquiringly. "Look at the drape of my mother's skirt where it meets the floor. Doesn't that shoe look odd?"

Mrs. Ogilve examined the photo. "I expect it is just the fold of the dress."

"No. There was something about my mother's shoes." Cate searched back in memory but she could not remember what it was.

"Perhaps something else in these papers will jog your memory," Mrs. Ogilve suggested.

Setting the photo where she could see it as she worked, Cate turned back to the open case. In one packet she found tickets for Susannah and Alexander McLaren to sail from Detroit, Michigan to Buffalo, New York, take the train from Buffalo to New York City and sail from New York City to Dover, England, along with hotel reservations in New York and London and a $5,000 international letter of credit.

Tied in a bundle were bank and stock account statements for Susannah and Alexander McLaren. Next she examined a small ledger with pages of names, dates and dollar sums with question marks after many names, and a large envelope containing 73 letters in foreign languages signed by Alexander D. McLaren, Secretary Treasurer of the German & Slovenian Miners Bank. The bank stationary listed Frederick M. Meyer as President and Alexander D. McLaren as Secretary Treasurer.

A small, leather bound, New Testament was the last item in the case.

"All of these things belong to Alexander McLaren, not to my father." Cate said when the briefcase was empty.

Mrs. Ogilve did not respond. She was beginning to regret finding the case.

"Maybe this belonged to an uncle or a friend and my father was keeping it for him," Cate sighed sinking back against the chair. "No, that doesn't make sense either. If I had an uncle, I would have gone to live with him when my mother died."

Mrs. Ogilve leaned forward. "Catherine, when you asked me earlier if I had told you everything we knew about your father and your background I said we had. I did not, however, add that Rev. Ogilve and I came to doubt that your father had been totally truthful with us."

"No, you did not tell me that."

"There wasn't anything to tell because we had no facts. We did strongly feel, however, that your father's love for you was quite genuine and it was obvious that you felt the same towards him.

"We concluded there had been some trouble or danger, something your father thought he could take care of and then return for you. He seemed a good man and Rev. Ogilve thoroughly expected he would return. I expect that is why he put the case away and never opened or mentioned it."

Sad and troubled, Cate asked, "You said Rev. Ogilve thought he would return. What did you think?"

"I was unsure. But, after seeing the contents of this case, I think Donald was right, as he so often was."

"You do?"

"Yes, I do. These papers may be some sort of proof your father had of wrongdoing. Look at the list that has the question marks. They are drawn with sharp emphasis and some have two or three on the same line, very different from the other pages. And look at this letter signed by Alexander McLaren; the handwriting does not appear to be the same as that in the notebook. Perhaps the notebook belonged to your father and the other things to Alexander McLaren."

"You think so?" Cate asked, as hope began to rise.

"It is a possibility," Mrs. Ogilve responded.

Cate looked at the papers spread over the table. She picked up the small leather-bound New Testament, unsnapped the clasp and opened the front cover. There, inscribed in elegant, scrolled handwriting was:

Presented to
Alexander Duncan McLaren
on the 16th day of May 1834
In recognition of his Conformation into
God's Church

**Go now into the great world ever keeping
God's Word in your heart
from
The Reverend John Lowell Avery
Prosters Home For Orphan Boys
Boston, Massachusetts**

"Alexander Duncan McLaren. Alexander Duncan. He just dropped the last name and I was too young to know the difference!

"All these years I kept hoping and praying that some day my father would return. My knight in shining armor!" Cate tossed the New Testament on to the table in disgust.

"Do not judge too quickly, Catherine. We do not know what these things mean."

"No. But we certainly know what they look like." Keeping only the photograph, she jammed everything else back into the brief case and shoved it across the table to Mrs. Ogilve. Mrs. Ogilve gently pushed it back.

"Catherine, these things belong to you. You must keep them for they may be very important. Also, there is the money. I'm sure your father wanted you to have it. That is why he left it, so you would be taken care of if he did not return."

"No." Cate spoke harshly. "You should take it, you need it now. Besides, think of all you spent raising me."

"Young lady," Mrs. Ogilve's voice snapped back at Cate, "how we spent our money, and on whom, was our business, not yours, not anyone's." Her voice softened. "I do not need the money. You know I am going to live with Peter and Hulda in Chicago. Peter has more money than he can ever spend and I will be well taken care of. No, I am fine. It is you that I am worried about."

"Me?" Cate was insulted. "I can support myself. I've been offered a teaching position at the Latin School for Girls in Harrisburg, Pennsylvania. Surely, you did not think I expected you to support me?"

Harriet stood and began clearing the dishes. She needed a moment to think.

"I'm not worried about you supporting yourself, Catherine, but rather about how you feel about what we found today. When your father did not return you were a very angry child. It was not easy, but over the years you gradually buried the past and grew into a lovely young woman.

"If we had not found this case perhaps it all would have stayed buried but we have found it, and I see it brings back great pain and anger."

"Wouldn't you be angry if you found something like this about your father?" Cate challenged.

"Yes, until I thought of my father's character and then I'd know there was more to the story. I only met your father that one time, still, he did not seem a wicked man. I know appearances can be deceiving but what cannot be faked is the love of a child. You loved your father, Catherine, loved him and trusted him."

"Yes, and a lot of good it did me! He dumped me and disappeared."

"Perhaps. But now he seems to have reappeared. Not exactly in the manner you had hoped but, nevertheless, here he is. Do you not think you ought to give him a chance to explain what happened?"

"And just how can he do that?"

"Read through the papers carefully before you jump to a conclusion. I noticed the passports and some of the other papers had addresses in Red Jacket, Michigan. Perhaps you should go to Red Jacket and see if the answers to your questions are there."

"What about the teaching position in Harrisburg?"

"Have you agreed to take it?"

"No. But I must decide by the 16th."

"Was this a position you particularly wanted?"

"The head of the music department at Oberlin thought it was an outstanding opportunity but I'm not sure I want to teach at a girls school. I thought I would teach in a public school."

"Then the girls school in Harrisburg would not be the correct position for you in any case. I would suggest that you write immediately informing them you cannot accept the position. There is more than enough money in the case to support you while find out what these papers mean and look for another position."

"Supposing I spend all the money and still don't know what the papers mean, or where my father is?"

'Well," laughed Mrs. Ogilve, "you said you do not want the money anyway."

Cate smiled sheepishly, acknowledging her contrariness before saying, "And if I secure a teaching position in Red Jacket, I might not have to use much of that money. I really want to teach in a public school. Why not there?"

Once her mind was made up, Cate acted quickly. That evening she wrote to The Latin School For Girls and the following day accompanied Mrs. Ogilve to Chicago. She planned to stay overnight with Hulda and Peter before leaving for the north but Hulda insisted she stay for several days in order to receive their surprise graduation present. The family dressmaker was to make a complete wardrobe for Cate.

"After all," said Hulda, "as a school teacher you will need smart looking, well wearing everyday clothes and, if you are to be invited out in society, you must wear clothes of quality and style. Mrs. Safranski will be with us for several days, and she will have you outfitted in no time at all."

Hulda personally oversaw the selections of materials and styles and, as she did so, Cate discovered an intelligent and humorous woman she had not known before. For as long as she could remember Cate had felt unwelcome in Peter and Hulda's home, but on this visit they were warm and welcoming. Cate wondered if it was because Mrs. Ogilve was going to be living with them and they wanted her to feel free to visit the woman who had become her mother. Whatever the reason, Cate was relieved to know she would be welcomed when she came to visit Mrs. Ogilve.

Finally, with tears and hugs and building excitement, Cate boarded the train to Red Jacket, Michigan. Taking a seat by the window, she made herself comfortable in the noisy, swaying, railroad car, and as they chugged north past small towns and cultivated farms she felt she was rushing toward adventure. The train skirted the shores of Lake Michigan until shortly past Milwaukee it entered seemingly unending forests of hemlock and white pine that continued until Cate arrived in Red Jacket.

In those long hours from Chicago to the top of Michigan's Upper Peninsula, Cate tried to remember traveling the other way, from Red Jacket to Grand Falls but it was all a blank. Her memories started with her father leaving her at the Ogilves.

She remembered how confused and lonely she felt waiting for him to come back and, when he did not return, the bargains she tried to make with God. If I do very well in school, father will come. When that did not work she changed it to, if I do everything perfectly, he will be so proud he will hurry back. Constant disappointment gradually created a desire to hurt him. How embarrassed he would be when he saw how well she had done, and how shamefully he had neglected her. Oh, deep would be his remorse, and great her satisfaction as he pleaded for her forgiveness. That fantasy stayed the longest, but it too finally disappeared. She was uncomfortably aware that it was rising again.

After all, she wondered, what do I think I'm going to find? My father? And if I find him? What if he is perfectly well and just did not care enough to come for me? What then?

Or supposing I find that he was not my father, but just someone who stole me away from my parents? Or that he is a criminal, and has been in prison all these years. It could be the money I have is stolen money, and when he gets out of prison he will come looking for it. What do I do then? Do I really want to know what all the papers mean?

And when I get there, what then? How am I going to find out anything? Am I going to stop people on the street and say, "Oh, pardon me, but can you give me answers to something that may, or may not, have happened here 15 years ago?"

Cate laughed at herself. It makes no sense rushing off like this, but it feels right. It feels exciting and right. And if I don't find the answers, I won't be any worse off than I am now. She sighed, closed her eyes and napped on the bouncing, swaying train.

Chapter 4

Dear Mrs. Ogilve,

    I have arrived safely and taken a room at the Calumet Hotel. The hotel was recommended by a classmate from Oberlin, James Wright, who, much to my surprise came walking thorough the train shortly after we left Chicago,

    Another surprise was that his home is in Red Jacket. I told him that was my destination. He inquired as to whom I was visiting. When I said I was not visiting anyone, he, of course, wanted to know, "Why was I traveling to Red Jacket?" I was hard put to answer. I had not thought about people asking me questions, just about the questions I was going to ask them!

    He must have decided the music department at Oberlin had not arranged a teaching position for me, and that I was going to a booming mining area to try my luck because he made rather a 'do' of pointing out that the local schools are growing and that teachers, perhaps even music teachers, are needed.

    He gave me the name of the superintendent of schools, Dr. Weissmiller, and said he would be *honored if I used his name as a reference. Was that not most kind of him?*

I am sure it was a great help to have Mr. Wright as a local reference because I wrote to Dr. Weissmiller this morning right after I checked into the hotel and he responded by the afternoon mail! I have an appointment to meet with him tomorrow. Truly, I could not imagine an immediate response without Mr. Wright's reference.

Red Jacket is an interesting town. I walked around quite a bit today just to see what is here and was impressed by the variety of stores and the large number of homes. One of the strangest things about it is that we are so far north that though it is now ten o'clock at night the sun is just beginning to set.

I thought of you often on the journey north and miss you already. Do write and let me know how things are with you.

> *Affectionately Yours,*
> *Catherine*

Cate smiled. To everyone else I'm Cate, but to Mrs. Ogilve, I will always be "Catherine, because that is your name."

In the morning Cate dressed carefully for the interview selecting a dark blue skirt with matching jacket. It was nice to wear beautiful clothes she had to admit as she turned slowly in front of the mirror to be sure that from the top of her sky-blue bonnet to the bottom of her high-button shoes all was neat and tidy. Once again she had won the battle to subdue her long red hair and achieve the professional look a school teacher was expected to have. When others envied her lovely long curls she smiled and said nothing of the daily battle to brush out the tangles those lovely natural curls turned into at night.

Upon leaving the hotel, Cate looked around, pleased that Red Jacket did not seem to be like the wild, ramshackle mining towns featured in newspapers. The hotel clerk told her over 12,000 people lived there with another 30,000 in surrounding towns and new people arriving every day. Two and three-story buildings lined the main streets and there was a heady feeling of industry and progress in the air. Businessmen, housewives, miners and laborers moved along the sidewalks while horse-drawn wagons and buggies clattered through the streets day and night.

Cate was happily surprised and impressed when she saw Lincoln High School. It was an attractive three-story brick building, big enough to accommodate 1,200 students, a large library, and modern laboratories.

Dr. Benjamin Weissmiller came forward to meet Cate when she entered his office. Slight of stature and tending towards plumpness, he possessed a happy zest for life and immediately put Cate at ease.

"Miss Duncan! Do come in and be seated." He ushered Cate to a comfortable chair by his desk. Smiling pleasantly, he said, "I understand you are inquiring about a position in our music department?"

"Yes, Dr. Weissmiller. If you have an opening."

Dr. Weissmiller nodded. "Strangely, I do. I say strangely, that is, because a week ago I was fully staffed. As you are no doubt aware, had I known we were going to need a music teacher we would have gone to the colleges seeking one. That is the normal procedure. But, unexpectedly we do need a teacher, in fact a music teacher, and suddenly you appear with a recommendation from one of our finest graduates, James Wright.

"Your application states you graduated from Oberlin. Fine college, Oberlin. We've sent a number of our students there. Is that where you made Mr. Wright's acquaintance?"

"Yes, Mr. Wright and I both graduated from Oberlin two weeks ago."

"Excellent. Excellent. Would you happen to have your diploma with you?" Expecting the question Cate handed over her diploma.

"Fine, excellent. Of course, I will make inquiries at the college but everything looks in order. Meanwhile, I expect you would like to know about the position Mr. Bignuenet vacated when he suddenly left the area last week. Why he left without giving us proper notice is a mystery and most inconvenient.

"Nevertheless, we are now in need of a music teacher for the Hawthorne, Longfellow and Washington elementary schools. Our elementary music teachers work mainly in the choral area and in English because many of our students come to school with little or no English. Choral work helps them with the language and it is a happy activity for children. Not only that, but choral work lends itself well to public performance and the parents enjoy it whether or not they understand English.

"I do not know if you realize it, Miss Duncan, but native-born Americans are a minority of the population here, very much a minority, only 30 to 40 percent. You will hear many different languages, German, French, Finnish, Slovenian, Italian, and Polish are the more common ones. In some families the children are the only ones who learn to speak English."

"But doesn't that isolate the women in their homes?" Cate asked.

"No, not really," Dr. Weissmiller responded. "The different nationalities tend to group together and create their own neighborhoods and the women soon learn which stores have clerks that speak their particular language. Speaking of languages, which ones have you studied, Miss Duncan?"

"In High School, Latin and German and at Oberlin, two years of Latin and one year of German and French. I also know some Italian from my vocal studies."

"Were those courses required by the music department?"

"No, the English Department. I also received an English diploma."

"Well, now, that is most interesting. I'm puzzled as to why you did not mention your English diploma in your letter asking for a meeting?"

"I did not want to imply that I was seeking anything other than a music position." Cate smiled at Dr. Weissmiller. He did not smile back and Cate wondered if he had been an English teacher and if she had offended him.

"I see," said Dr. Weissmiller. "Well, in any case, our school year commences September 1, and terminates June 16. A beginning teacher's salary is $51.53 per month, August through May and half pay in June. Teachers are expected to be here for meetings three weeks before school starts in September."

Cate stood at the window of her hotel thinking about the interview. It seemed to have gone well, but... Well, there's no sense worrying about it. He'll hire me or he won't. And if I don't get that job I'll find something else because I'm staying right here. I came to find out about my father and that is what I'm going to do. So I better find a boardinghouse and get out of this expensive hotel.

The desk clerk told Cate where she could purchase a copy of the *The Copper Mining Gazette* and armed with the Rooms to Let page she set off to find a boarding house. Everywhere she went she was told the room had been taken. It seemed odd that they should all be filled.

Her spirits rose walking up to the Lindstrom Family Boarding House. It looked clean and well kept with a profusion of flowers in the yard and "A Room To Let" sign in the window.

Mrs. Lindstrom answered the door. Cate commented on how pleasant the house looked and asked to be shown the vacant room. Standing firmly in the doorway, Mrs. Lindstrom said, "Absolutely not! No unmarried woman is going to cause trouble in my place."

Astonished, Cate said, "I assure you I am very respectable. I would never..."

"So you say." Scornfully she looked Cate up and down, "But then, that's what they all say." The door was closed firmly in Cate's face.

Shocked, Cate stood staring at the door, then slowly turned and walked away.

What was it James Wright had said on the train? "Be careful where you room. Red Jacket is a mining town and not like other places. It's noisy and, ah, miners come and go at all hours of the day and night and, ah, you'll want to find a quiet place." He had seemed embarrassed when he said that. Now she suspected she knew why. He was trying to tell her a woman coming to Red Jacket alone was at high risk of being considered 'not respectable'.

Cate laughed, "Me, a femme fatal! And to think I almost ended up in the ever-so-proper, ever-so-chaperoned, Latin School for Young Women in Harrisburg, Pennsylvania."

Now what do I do, Cate wondered turning back towards the hotel. Thoughtfully, she walked past dry goods stores, saloons, furniture and undertaking establishments, restaurants, saloons, grocery stores, banks, brokerages, insurance offices and more saloons. Saloons were busy day and night serving men and women.

In Great Falls there was one saloon and it was kept discretely out of sight behind the post office. The Presbyterian, Methodist, and Congregational churches all preached against the consumption of spirits and the priest at the Roman Catholic church was known to publicly reprimand problem drinkers.

At Oberlin, drinking was not permitted and students who did so were expelled. The feeling against drinking was so strong that when students heard a saloon was being built near the campus they tried to persuade the owner to take his business elsewhere. He ignored them. The night before the saloon was to open the students deconstructed the building. The owner arrived the next day to an empty lot. Disgusted, he finally took his trade elsewhere.

Cate suspected if students pulled such a stunt in Red Jacket they would be lynched, not lionized, as they had been at Oberlin.

Chapter 5

814 Hecla Avenue
Red Jacket, Michigan
June 22, 1885

Dear Mrs. Ogilve,

I cannot tell you how grateful I am that you encouraged me to attempt this adventure. I would not have had the courage to do it on my own. I suspect there are many things I would not have had the courage to do 'on my own' that you and Rev. Ogilve made possible for me. I do thank you.

I have not heard from Dr. Weissmiller about the teaching position. If the dean of the music school at Oberlin is taking a vacation before summer classes start it may be quite a while before he receives Dr. Weissmiller's letter and can respond to it. I must learn to be patient.

You may be amused to know that I solved my housing problem by imitating my father and seeking help from the clergy. After church service Sunday morning I introduced myself to Rev. & Mrs. Campbell and explained my situation. Mrs. Campbell insisted I accompany them home for an excellent dinner and they were most kind to me.

The next morning Mrs. Campbell wrote and suggested I call upon a Mrs. John Sincock. The

Sincock's children have all left home and Mrs. Sincock said, "The house is a lonely place with no young person in it."

I will board with the Sincocks, but Mrs. Sincock insists on calling me a guest. She is fearful people will think they need to take in boarders (something 'not done' on Hecla Avenue). Hecla Avenue is where successful mine managers and businessmen live. Mrs. Sincock was proud of the address and made sure I understood its significance.

It is pleasant three-story house with a wraparound porch. I think there are five bedrooms. Mine is a large corner room with three windows on the second floor. There is an excellent piano in the parlor I am free to use, in fact, encouraged to, as it was purchased for the children's piano lessons and neither Mr. nor Mrs. Sincock play.

Your upcoming trip to New York City with Hulda and Peter sounds wonderful. Will you include an evening at the Philharmonic, or two or three? The orchestra is reputed to be excellent. Perhaps you will hear one of the new Brahms or Tchaikovsky compositions. That would be exciting.

Do have a wonderful time.

> *Affectionately,*
> *Catherine*

Her housing problem settled, Cate decided to begin giving music lessons hoping that if she was earning her way she would not attract attention nor be labeled as a man hunter. She placed a notice in the newspaper stating she was available to give piano, organ and voice lessons and told Mrs. Sincock, the

Campbells and James Wright she was looking for students.

Now she could start looking for her father. Since arriving in Red Jacket whenever Cate walked around town she had looked for the German & Slovenian Miners Bank. She found the Calumet Bank, the First National Bank, the Merchants & Mechanics Bank, and the Copper Country Building and Loan Association but no German & Slovenian Miners Bank.

Wondering if she had misremembered the name, Cate examined her father's papers again. The name was correct and with it was the address, 601 Laurium Street.

At 601 Laurium Street, stenciled in gold on the door, was *The RED JACKET BANK,* underneath it in smaller letters, *President, Frederick M. Meyer.* Walking slowly past the two large windows that fronted the street she saw two clerks waiting on customers and three other employees working at desks. None of them looked old enough to be her father.

So, Cate thought, the business name has changed but Frederick Meyer is still there. Now, who do I ask about him? Mrs. Sincock?

Mrs. Sincock was in the kitchen rolling out pie dough.

"Cate! I'm so glad you came back early. I've been meaning to tell you the church picnic is tomorrow." She brushed back a stray lock of hair leaving a white flour smear on her cheek. "I do hope you can come with us. It will be a wonderful day. The picnic grounds are at the foot of the Red Cliffs. They are magnificent.

"But, now I must not waste time talking, I'm way behind with my baking. I've become so spoiled having a maid that I'm overwhelmed trying to do everything alone. Last week Freda asked for today off and without thinking I said yes but, oh, I wish she was here now."

Cate smiled and asked, "Could I help? Mrs. Ogilve taught me to cook and to bake."

"She did? How wonderful. Of course I couldn't ask you to help but if you would like to? Well, to start with, the hazel nuts need to be cracked and chopped. Oh, you are a dear. Aprons are in the top drawer on the left."

This was definitely not the time to ask Mrs. Sincock about Frederick Meyer, Cate decided as she began chopping nuts.

The following morning Mrs. Sincock and Cate carefully packed wicker picnic baskets with a large bowl of potato salad, two fried chickens, three jars of pickles, one chocolate cake with hazelnut frosting, two blueberry pies, two dozen frosted ginger cookies, a gallon of lemonade, a tablecloth, silverware, and dishes for three. Mr. Sincock carefully placed the baskets in the buggy and helped the ladies aboard.

It was a lovely day, sunny and warm with soft breezes. Cate was delighted with the hourlong ride to the picnic grounds through thick green woods so cool she shivered, and warm, sun bright meadows filled with wildflowers topped by the bright blue sky with white clouds that seemed to be racing the wind.

Finally, the Red Cliffs rose dramatically ahead and they soon reached the picnic grounds in a meadow at the foot of the cliffs. A stream ran along one side of the meadow, bushes and small trees hugged the base of the cliffs and trailed off on the sides of the meadow.

The tables were set up, the food laid out, the Lord's blessing asked, and the eating began. Mrs. Campbell waited until Cate had filled her plate from the wonderful selection of food and then said, "Come with me. The young people are sitting by themselves and this will be a good opportunity to introduce you to everyone."

Cate tried to remember each person's name but there were 30 or so in the group and the names came too quickly. Still, she did get some names. The petite Yeo twins, Pearl and Opal, with their beautiful black curls and teasing eyes; Maggie Loch, round, plump, cheerful, the unofficial leader of the group. Gordon Carne, tall, handsome, expensively dressed, and the Dunn brothers, Jamie and Don with their soft accents.

"Come sit by me," invited Maggie Loch. "I won't know your whole family history by the end of lunch, but I will surely try to."

Laughter greeted Maggie's remark as several chimed in, "Don't you believe her. She will get your whole history, and more, before lunch is over."

"Thank you," said Cate. "It's wonderful to be included when you are a stranger. Are you all longtime friends from this area?" By the time everyone told her how long they had known each other, where they were from and, sometimes, why they had come to Red Jacket, lunch was over. It was time to play games and Maggie Loch was puzzled that she had not asked Cate a single question.

Regaining control of the group Maggie declared, "We are not going to play those boring old games."

"But what shall be do?" asked Opal Yeo.

"Let do something different, something interesting." pleaded Pearl.

As the group debated what that would be, Cate slipped away to speak to Rev. and Mrs. Campbell.

"Here's Catherine," Rev. Campbell announced as Cate walked up. "How are you getting along now?"

"Wonderfully, thanks to you and Mrs. Campbell. The Sincocks are lovely people."

"Did you hear that, Janet?" Andrew Campbell asked his wife who was sitting right next to him. "Isn't it grand when things work out so well? I see you are meeting some of our young people. I hope that works out well, too," he added smiling.

"Now Andrew, don't you start matchmaking," scolded Mrs. Campbell.

Cate laughed. "According to Mrs. Sincock that is practically the purpose of these picnics."

"If that is so," Rev. Campbell smiled, "then there has been a lot of matchmaking because this is our 16th summer picnic."

"Sixteen?" Mrs. Campbell was surprised.

"Yes, dear, I looked it up yesterday. The first picnic was in 1869, the year the church was built. Gilbert Anderson was the minister then and having quite a hard time of it with so few families and so many single men in the area. He was not pleased with the drinking and gambling constantly tempting the gullible young men. Left an unusually complete record of his ministry from establishing the congregation in 1860 to constructing the building in 1869. Fascinating reading."

"What was the minister's name?" Cate asked, unsure she had heard it correctly.

"Anderson. Gilbert Anderson," Rev. Campbell repeated.

"Come on Cate. We are going to pick wild blueberries." Cate's new friends arrived and swept her off to the far end of the meadow where they divided up an odd assortment of containers.

As a newcomer, Cate was offered advice and instructions from several people. She smiled and appeared to be listening but heard little of what was said. Her mind was in a turmoil and she wanted to be alone to think. When everyone scattered to pick blueberries, Cate went by herself towards the cliffs.

Gilbert Anderson! That was the name of the minister who recommend the Ogilves to my father. I'm sure it was. I wrote down everything Mrs. Ogilve told me after we opened the brief case and I'm sure that was the name.

Slowly, Cate wandered through the scattered bushes and trees near the foot of the cliffs and into a small clearing. Suddenly she heard a growl, a deep growl.

Cate stopped and, barely moving her head, looked around. On her right the tangle of bushes gave way to small trees. On the left the ground rose sharply to the stone cliffs. About five feet ahead, a bear cub was eating chokecherries in a small chokecherry tree. The growl came again, louder, angry.

Cate stood frozen.

"Don't move forward." The words were soft, firm. "The mother bear is in the bushes. I'm about ten feet behind you. Walk backwards very, very slowly. Do not turn around and keep your hands to your sides."

Slowly, trembling, Cate put one foot behind the other and stepped back. She froze again unable to breathe.

"That's the way," the soft voice encouraged, "keep coming back."

A shallow breath, then slowly, step by step by step, she moved backward. Her neck and shoulder muscles tightened until they ached and her breathe caught in her throat as she waited for the smashing, crushing attack of the mother bear.

"Good. You are almost to me." A strong, warm hand clasped her hand and guided her to his side. It was Jamie Dunn. He smiled into her terrified eyes and said, "We'll keep walking backwards a bit more. She'll not bother us as long as we go away from her cub. There is a stand of trees a few feet back. Once we reach them it will be safe to turn around."

A few more steps and they reached the trees and turned to walk naturally. Cate's legs could hardly hold her up and she stumbled forward. Jamie caught her. "You're trembling. Here lean on me," he suggested, putting his arm around Cate's shoulder. His arm felt strong and good and Cate began to relax. The trembling stopped and self-consciously she moved away from Jamie's arm.

They returned to the meadow and sat at a picnic table.

"Thank you," Cate said, finally able to speak. "A hundred times, thank you. I was terrified and I had no idea what to do. I literally could not move. I always thought I was brave, even adventurous, but when I heard that sound ... I don't know what would have happened if you had not been there."

"Ah, well, it was nothing. But you will have to be a wee bit cautious when it comes to bear cubs. You can't just walk up to them. That is being too adventuresome by far." He smiled as he spoke. Cate had a great temptation to stare into his dark blue eyes.

"I wasn't walking up to the cub," she explained. "Well, I guess I was, but it was not intentional. I did not see it was there until I heard that growl."

"What were you looking at then? For surely, you walked straight towards it."

Cate was embarrassed to have been so foolish and now she feared she was about to sound stupid. "I wasn't seeing anything, I'm afraid. I was thinking."

"It must have been something very serious, then?"

"Yes. Yes, it was." Cate was relieved that he did not laugh at her and wondered if she should tell him what she had been thinking.

As Cate and Jamie sat talking, Maggie Loch and Gordon Crane came back into the meadow walking towards the picnic table. "Well, well." said Maggie. "Isn't our Cate a fast worker? With Jamie Dunn, no less, who is always too busy working to attend parties or take a girl to a dance."

"So I see," agreed Gordon. "I wonder if she knows Jamie is just a teamster at Charbonneau's lumber yard."

When they reached the table Maggie put their can of blueberries on the table and said, "You are the first ones back. You must have found a good patch of berries."

"I'm afraid I didn't pick any," Cate said and then explained about the mother bear and the cub. Jamie was an embarrassed hero as the story quickly spread and worried parents told their children they must stay in plain view in the meadow. There would to be no hide and seek among the bushes and trees today.

At supper time Rev. Campbell offered a prayer of thanksgiving for such a beautiful day, everyone joined in singing grace and then the hungry picnickers made sure picnic baskets returned to town empty.

At Cate's table conversation was about the upcoming 4th of July parade.

"I think the 4th of July parade is the best of the whole year," said Pearl Yeo.

"No, no," scoffed Gordon Carne. "St. Jean's Day Parade on midsummer's day is the best. The French Canadians really know how to have fun."

"Where's your loyalty?" asked Will Doolittle. "Any good Englishman knows it's the St. George's Day Parade."

"Loyalty to England?" Donnie Dunn was outraged. "I'm a Scot and I say St. Andrew's Day Parade is the best."

"What about St. Joseph's Society Parade?" asked Edgar Vertin, sticking up for his Slovenian heritage.

"Don't forget the St. Patrick's Day parade." Hector Foley jumped into the conversation. "That's my favorite." The opinions flew back and forth. Soon it was nine o'clock and everyone gathered together to sing "Blest Be The Tie That Binds". It was a delightful, peaceful moment and the picnic was over.

Jamie and Cate carried the Sincock's baskets to their buggy.

"I've never heard of so many parades," Cate said as they walked along. "How do people have time to go to work?"

Jamie laughed. "Well, not everyone goes to all the parades. I only go on the 4th of July. It is better than all the rest combined because it is for everyone. The other parades are all right, but they carry on the old ways and the old prejudices. I don't much care for sticking to the old ways in a new country. If I wanted that I would have stayed in Canada."

"Is Canada your home?" Cate asked.

"No. This is my home. I've taken out my first citizenship papers and one day I will be a citizen." He spoke with a quiet confidence. "But I expect you really were asking if I was a Canadian? And to that the answer is yes. I was born and raised in Kincardin, Ontario. My parents migrated there from Scotland."

Which explained his soft accent, Cate thought as they arrived at the buggy. Jamie placed the baskets in the buggy, gave Cate a hand up, said goodbye to the Sincocks and to

Cate, adding, "I'll look forward to seeing you at the 4th of July Parade, Miss Duncan."

Cate watched him walk away. She liked the way he walked with an easy balance and strength. She liked the way the evening sun cast gold highlights on his dark brown hair.

Watching Cate watch Jamie, Anna Sincock smiled. "You seem to have made a friend?" she commented.

Cate did not respond to the half question but she wondered if Mrs. Sincock was right.

Back at the house Cate hurried to her room to check her notes for Gilbert Anderson's name. It was there and he was the minister that recommend the Ogilves to her father!

Thoughtfully, she put the case away. So some of what my father said was true. There was a Rev. Anderson but he was in Michigan, not Illinois. And there is a Frederick Meyer but no German and Slovenian Miners Bank. It's as if everything he said is half-true.

What do I know that is true? I know my mother taught me to play the piano because Mrs. Ogilve says I told her that when I first arrived and a five-year-old child would not make up piano lessons. And I know that my mother is dead. Or do I? Do I really know she's dead?

As she thought about it Cate remembered Rev. Campbell's comments about the church records.

Chapter 6

Cate woke up the following morning eager to search the church records but when she arrived at the First Presbyterian Church Rev. Campbell was not there. He was away at a meeting of the Presbytery and he would not return until the weekend.

Disappointed, Cate returned to the Sincocks where she was pleased to discover a letter had arrived in the morning mail.

3 Miscowaubik Street
Red Jacket, Michigan
June 25, 1885

Dear Miss Duncan,
Please call at my home this morning at eleven o'clock to discuss piano lessons for my daughters.
Sincerely yours,
Martha Gribble

"I seem to have found my first pupils," Cate said, handing the letter to Mrs. Sincock who had been hovering about obviously interested in Cate's letter.

"Oh, you are lucky," she exclaimed. "This is from Martha Gribble."

Cate was puzzled by Mrs. Sincock's reaction. "Is this Martha Gribble someone special?"

"Is she someone special! Child, she is Mrs. Nathaniel Gribble, the most important woman in Red Jacket. Mr. Gribble is head of Miscowaubik and Boston, the most important mining company on the Keweenaw Peninsula."

"Isn't that where Mr. Sincock works?"

"It is. And it is a fine company to work for, I can tell you."

Mrs. Sincock paused as the maid, Freda Kaisa, entered the parlor and carefully set down a tray holding a coffee pot, cream and sugar, two cups and saucers and a plate of sugar cookies.

"Thank you, Freda. I was just going to ask you to add a second cup for Miss Duncan and here you have already thought of it."

Mrs. Sincock looked around and sighed contentedly. "Sometimes I still can't believe our good fortune. We did not live like this when we first came from Cornwall. Many times we barely had enough to eat and the mining camps were rough and tumble shanty towns. And the miners," she shook her head remembering, "not all of them, mind you, but some, when they got liquored up, would fight each other, smash up the bars and no woman was safe on the street until they sobered up.

But the worst was that so many mines failed. And left the miners with no wages and no work.

"When Mr. Sincock started with the Miscowaubik, it was a hole in the ground. A big hole surrounded by woods. There were no railroads to Red Jacket in those days. There weren't even roads!"

"Can you imagine trying to build a mine and a town in a place where everything had to be shipped in by boat? And then, when Lake Superior froze, as it does every winter, nothing could be shipped until spring. If you ran out of dynamite for the mine or flour for your family it was just too bad for you.

"But, when the Boston people sent Nathaniel Gribble here to run the Miscowaubik Mine, things began to change. He knew what he was doing and how to be ready for the winter freeze. He was the one who got the mine shafts sunk, the stamp mills constructed, and the roads and railroads built. The company began to grow and the town too.

"Mr. Sincock grew right along with the company because Mr. Gribble looked for honest, hardworking men who knew how to solve problems. John started out as a mechanic. Now he is the Superintendent of Surface Operations at the Miscowaubik and we live in this fine house."

She paused to sip her coffee.

"Our first home here was log cabin. Why even Mrs. Gribble lived in a log cabin hotel her first summer here. Well, it called itself a hotel but it was so poorly built that you could see daylight though the logs. And Red Jacket was so rough and dangerous that Mrs. Gribble never left the hotel without a gun strapped to her waist. Soon as summer ended she went back to Boston. I was surprised she returned the next summer I can tell you."

Suitably impressed with Mrs. Gribble's importance, Cate dressed with particular care for the interview, wearing a light brown summer dress and a flat straw hat with a matching color band. Then, armed with directions from Mrs. Sincock, Cate took her time walking the six blocks to the Gribble residence. The temperature was rising into the 80's and she did not think arriving with perspiration dripping down her face would make a good impression on 'the most important woman in town'.

The Gribble home was impressive. Set well back from the street, the large three-story house, with bay windows, corner turrets and a wide, covered porch sweeping across the front and around the sides, presented a sense of elegance and welcome.

A maid escorted Cate along the dark center hall to the music room. "What a cheerful room," Cate thought stepping from the dark hall into a brightly lit room. Four large windows let in the light and a colorful velvet carpet and pastel wallpaper gave it an elegant look.

"Do come in, Miss Duncan." Setting aside her reading glasses, Mrs. Gribble welcomed Cate. "I am Martha Gribble and I have heard such nice things about you from Mr. Wright. He tells me you are a pianist and organist of unusual ability."

Embarrassed, Cate felt the color rise in her cheeks. "Mr. Wright is much too kind."

"Is he?" Martha smiled. "Well, in any case, I am looking for someone to give lessons in both instruments. Our parlor organ is small and not of the best quality but it should be adequate for beginning lessons.

"Both of our daughters play the piano. They have their lesson books with them and are supposed to practice throughout the summer but they don't. When we return to Boston in the fall their teacher is unhappy. I'm quite sure regular lessons will give them the incentive to practice.

"Nette is our youngest daughter. She is eleven-years old and loves music but, I must confess, she has inherited my lack of talent. Nevertheless, as long as she wishes to continue lessons, she may.

"Emma is fourteen and she is the talented one. It does not seem to matter what it is, languages, music, science, she masters them all with little effort. The organ lessons will be for her."

Martha Gribble picked up a small bell and rang it, summoning the maid who was sent to fetch Nette and Emma.

Nette, a thin, freckle-faced child with straight brown hair and sparkling brown eyes hurried eagerly into the room. Cate liked her immediately.

Emma, looking bored, followed soon after. She was astonishingly beautiful. Cate had seen other young women with lovely black hair, dark blue eyes and perfect complexions, but none as arresting as Emma.

The lessons were scheduled for Tuesday and Thursday mornings at 9 and 10 o'clock.

Lesson times settled, Mrs. Gribble invited Cate to attend a musical evening at the Gribble home Friday evening.

"We have quite a number of talented singers and musicians in Red Jacket and in the surrounding towns who enjoy performing. This will be a good opportunity for you to meet them. James Wright and his sister, Erma, will be here. Do come around 8 o'clock."

Cate was delighted to accept the invitation.

The first guest to arrive on Friday evening was Florence Meyer. Martha Gribble sighed knowing that Florence would undoubtedly begin her conversation with, "How pleasant it is to converse with a cultured Bostonian." Florence firmly believed that because she was from Boston she was culturally and socially superior to almost everyone in the United States, much less, Red Jacket.

"Where is Frederick this evening?" Martha asked hoping to divert the boring cant.

"Attending a banker's meeting in Detroit. I expect him home tomorrow."

"Good evening, Mrs. Gribble. Mrs. Meyer." Both ladies faces lit up as Louis Pouline presented himself with a half bow. Suave, handsome, 28 years old and unmarried, Louis was a charmer. He knew it and capitalized on it carefully maintaining his southern accent and manners. He had left the South's post Civil War poverty to make his fortune in the North. It had been a good decision. In just three years he had risen from clerk to Treasurer of The Red Jacket Miners Bank.

Emma and Nette joined the group. "Hello Mrs. Meyer. Hello Mr. Pouline." Nette said quickly, then without waiting for a reply turned to her mother, "Mama? Don't you think Miss Duncan is beautiful? Don't you?"

"Really, Nette. You are such a child." Emma's voice dripped the scorn. "It is a well-known fact that redheads are never beautiful, their complexions are much too pale."

"But Miss Duncan's complexion is not pale. It's not!" Nette insisted. "She's beautiful. Isn't she, Mama?"

Smiling fondly at her daughters, Martha Gribble said, "I think I must agree with Nette. Miss Duncan's complication is lovely and she is a very attractive young woman."

"Mr. Pouline will agree with me, I'm sure," said Emma with a dramatic coyness that disturbed her mother.

"Alas, I must beg off for I have not met Miss Duncan and, surely, I would be a cad to disparage a lady's appearance." Louis smiled at Emma as he spoke and she sighed and smiled back, lost in his soft New Orleans drawl.

Martha Gribble unconsciously narrowed her eyes and silently determined to keep a very close watch on Mr. Pouline and her obviously smitten daughter.

Observing Emma sigh and Martha's reaction, Florence Meyer felt a tickle of malicious delight. "And who," she asked, "is Miss Duncan?"

June 28, 1885

Dear Mrs. Ogilve,

The music lessons with the Gribble girls have begun well. The youngest, Nette, comes skipping into the music room smiling and ready to play. She does not have a natural touch but she practices diligently and her skills will grow.

The older sister, Emma, has a wonderful talent. She expresses deep feelings and emotions when playing the piano and will do very well with the organ. Away from the instruments, she seems rather cold but that may change as I become better acquainted with her.

Tonight I attended a musical evening at the Gribble home. It was a large gathering, forty or more, and I will have to struggle to remember all of the new names and faces. James Wright, my friend from Oberlin, and his sister, Erma, were my kind escorts. They sang a lovely duet and I so enjoyed their conversation that I'm confident Erma, along with James, will be my friend.

The musical highlight of the evening was Franklin Ogden's piano playing. Mr. Ogden is the organist at the 5th Street Methodist church. He studied at the Boston Conservatory and is acquainted with two of my Oberlin music professors. He said he greatly misses living in Boston and attending concerts. I told him you were going to attend the New York Philharmonic and promised to let him know what compositions were performed.

I begin to think that Mrs. Gribble has taken me under her wing. Not only did she invite me to her home this evening, but now she has invited me to join the family at their 4th of July celebration and requested Mr. Louis Pouline to escort me. I suspect that Mr. Pouline was as surprised as I was by her request. We had just been introduced this evening and really did not have much conversation together. I do hope she is not matchmaking!

Monday, Rev. Campbell will show me the church records. I expect he finds my interest in old church records rather odd but he is a kind man and does not question me.

> With Great Affection,
> Catherine

Chapter 7

Settled at a table in the church basement Cate sent a silent prayer to God before carefully opening the 1860 - 1870 record book of the First Presbyterian Church. The trials and success of Rev. Anderson's days in Red Jacket were written in diary form with periodic breaks for lists of baptisms, marriages, confirmations, deaths and expenses. Cate searched for her parents' names. Hers should be there also, when she was baptized.

When Cate passed her birth year and her name did not appear in the baptismal record she stopped. Was there any point in going on? Sighing she decided to continue to the end, to 1870 the year she was left at the Ogilves.

And there, under Building Fund Contributors, she found Alexander Duncan McLaren, $1,000 and in parenthesis, (This handsome contribution is given by Mr. McLaren in gratitude to the Presbyterian Prosters Home For Orphan Boys.).

There! Finally. She had begun to wonder if she was chasing the wind. But no, here was proof she had come to the right area.

That had to be her father. The Prosters Home For Orphan Boys was the convincing fact. But she had found nothing about her mother, nothing about herself.

Cate returned the records to Rev. Campbell and left the church. Outside Jamie Dunn was unloading 2 by 4's destined for a Sunday School shelving project. She stopped by his wagon and laughed when she saw how surprised he looked when he turned and saw her waiting there.

Eyes twinkling, Jamie said, "Good morning, Miss Duncan. May I offer you a ride in my elegant carriage."

"Aren't you supposed to be very busy?" Cate teased.

"I am. Indeed, I am. But, into all life some sunshine must fall. Whoops. I think I should have said some sun must shine."

They laughed and Cate asked, "Are you on your way back to the lumberyard?"

"No. We are short of drivers today so I'm helping with deliveries. I'm on my way to the cemetery with a load of fence poles. I don't suppose you'd like to come along."

There was a long silence as Cate thought about it. Finally, she said, "Yes. I would."

Jamie looked surprised and pleased as he helped her up on to the wagon seat. Then climbing up himself, he shook the reins and directed the horses onto the street, skillfully maneuvering through the heavy traffic.

By the time they reached less traveled roads, Cate seemed lost in thought. Finally, Jamie cleared his throat and asked. "Are you sure you want to go to the cemetery?"

"What? Oh, yes," Cate responded, embarrassed to think she had been so wrapped up in her own thoughts that she had totally ignored him. No wondered he looked puzzled. But what to say?

"I'm sorry to be so rude," Cate began.

"No, you weren't rude," Jamie interrupted.

"Yes I was. I was rude and I shouldn't have been. But you see..." Cate paused, fumbling for words. "You are going to think this is extremely strange I'm sure, but the reason I want to go to the cemetery is .... is that I think my mother may be buried there and..."

Jamie's voice softened. "You have not been to the cemetery?"

"No."

"Well, no wonder you don't feel like talking. No, it is proper and right that you are solemn." He nodded his head sympathetically and Cate was relieved that he did not ask questions.

At the cemetery Cate got off at the caretaker's shack and Jamie continued on to unload the fence posts. The caretaker was old and hard of hearing but once he understood the name she was seeking he gave her excellent directions.

Her path led along a winding road, under shade trees. Benches were placed under some of the trees. Cate's steps slowed as she neared her mother's grave. And then she was in front of the large stone marker.

McLaren

Susannah Meyer McLaren
Beloved Wife and Mother
October 12, 1835 – July 10, 1870

Alexander Duncan McLaren
Beloved Husband and Father
May 9, 1837 – July 10, 1870

Catherine Alexandra McLaren
Beloved Daughter
September 30, 1865 – July 10, 1870

"Miss Duncan?"

Cate wasn't sure how long she had been standing, staring at the names when Jamie spoke. "I don't mean to rush you but I must return to the yard."

"I'm ready," said Cate, walking quickly away from the monument.

It took all of Cate's self-control to carry on a conversation with Jamie as he drove her back to the Sincocks.

When she was finally alone Cate sat and thought. And wondered, how could the tombstone say I'm dead? That my father is dead? And if I'm alive does that mean my mother is too?

Oh, it doesn't make sense. If Mrs. Ogilve hadn't said that was my father and me in the photograph I would think I just had the wrong name. But that couldn't be because the New Testament from the orphanage and the visas that belong to the man in the photograph are the same as on the tombstones. And the man in the photograph is my father.

But I am not dead! And if my father and I are not buried there, who is?

Cate did not like where her thoughts were taking her. Nothing she was discovering made her feel anything but confused and angry.

Well, I don't have to keep looking. I can stop. Nothing says that I must continue, does it? No one here even knows I'm looking for something.

That evening, exhausted and confused, Cate went to bed early and fell into a troubled, restless sleep. Toward morning she dreamt a long-forgotten dream.

She and her mother were sitting side by side on a piano bench. They were playing the piano in a room filled with bright sunlight. The music was lovely. Her mother smiled and nodded as Cate's small hands moved over the keys and Cate felt warm and safe and happy.

Then darkness crept into the room, covering the rug and the drapes, smothering the beautiful light. The piano and her mother disappeared and Cate was running. She ran and ran away from the dark. From the dark and from the red that terrified her, leaping at her, grabbing for her feet, threatening to trap her. She ran, gasping for breath as the red gained until---she woke up with her heart pounding.

It had been years since she had dreamed that dream but now she remembered it. Remembered how she would wake in the night, alone, afraid, confused, wanting her parents. Wanting to know why was she alone.

All those years of wondering and now, when I may be able to find out why, am I going to quit just because I might not like the answer? No. It doesn't matter if like the answers, it matters that I find them.

And, isn't it unusual for three members of a family to die on the same day? Diphtheria could kill three in a family but not all on the same day. No, it must have been something unusual, something that might be reported in a newspaper.

In the morning Cate went to *The Red Jacket Mining Gazette Newspaper* office and asked if they kept copies of old newspapers. They did and if she was willing to go to the basement and help Rufus Bloy, the elderly office clerk, look, he would see if they could find what she wanted. The basement was dark, dusty and poorly lit. Rufus led Cate to the shelves of old papers.

"In past times we were not always a daily newspaper." he explained. "So we may have to choose from the closest date. What was it exactly?"

"July 10, 1870 is the date."

"Here we are. Well, good news, we were a daily by then. Here's July 10, 11 and 12. I'll carry these upstairs for you. It is much too dark to see down here."

Mr. Bloy settled Cate at a desk with good light. She began with the July 11th issue.

COLLINS WAS MURDERED
KRECTZ INJURED IN MINE ACCIDENT
SMUGGLING PAYS BETTER
DEMAND FOR FARM LANDS
JOCKEY CHARGED WITH THEFT
EXPLOSION ON STEAM LAUNCH

The explosion on a steam launch occurred on the Mississippi and had nothing to do with her family. Then she opened the July 12, 1870 newspaper. Across the front page spread the headline

TRAGIC FIRE DESTROYS PROMINENT FAMILY

Red Jacket is stunned by the tragic fire that took the lives of Alexander McLaren, his wife Susannah McLaren, and their five-year-old daughter, Catherine.

The fire was discovered by Frederick Meyer as he was returning to his home from an evening card game. He saw the flames from the road and attempted to enter the house but, unable to do so, he raced to town for help.

The cause of the fire is unknown. The stately McLaren mansion, one of the finest homes in the area, was engulfed in flames when the firemen arrived. The valiant firemen attempted again and again to approach the house but the heat drove them back. The carriage house was also a total loss.

The friends and family members of Elsie Sotaniemi and Marta Charbonneau will be relieved to know that neither servant was in residence at the time of the fire.

The McLarens will be sorely missed by this community. Mrs. McLaren was known for her gracious manner to all and for her remarkable musical talents. Mr. McLaren was the best example of the self-made man who, though highly successful, never thought himself above others and was always the first to contribute to a destitute miner's widow or to a family that had lost their possessions in a fire.

The funeral will be at 2 o'clock on Saturday at the Evangelical Lutheran Church on Gay Street, in Red Jacket. Funeral arrangements are being handled by James Severtin.

Cate, making notes of the names and details, was surprised to see that the funeral was at a Lutheran Church. Coming up behind her, Rufus Bloy leaned over her shoulder looking at the newspaper. "Found what you were looking for, did you?" he said emitting strong fumes of liquor and garlic. "July 12th. Big fire on the front page. That the one you're looking at?"

Taking Cate's lack of denial as a yes, he went on, "That happened the first year I worked for this paper. I remember it, all right. Terrible, terrible tragedy. Whole family lost. Everything destroyed. Lots of rumors around that one."

Cate and Rufus eyed each other. Finally, she asked, "What kind of rumors?"

Rufus laughed. "That was what you were looking at. I thought so." He straightened up, grabbed a nearby chair and sat down, obviously wanting to talk. "Ever since you walked into the office to place that advertisement, I've been wondering who you reminded me of. It just kept nagging me. Then a few minutes ago it came to me. You look like her," he nodded toward the newspaper. "You're her niece, right?"

Cate, relieved that she could breathe again now that Rufus and his whisky breath were no longer in her face, ignored his question and asked hers again, "What were the rumors?"

"Well, first off the firemen said an occupied house with adults in it who would of been awake at that time of night, doesn't just burn all the way down like that without anyone getting out, and the barn, too, which was not that close to the house, not unless someone helped it along and the people in the house were unconscious or trapped.

"And then," he added smugly, "there was the clerk who, earlier on the night of the fire, told his buddies at the saloon there'd been a big dust up that day between Alex McLaren and Fred Meyer."

"What was the argument about?" Cate asked.

"Don't know. The clerk didn't say what they argued about when he first told us and then, the next day when he knew McLaren was dead he denied ever saying they'd argued."

"Why would he do that?"

"Well, he had a family to support and Meyer was his boss. He didn't want to lose his position and Meyer was known as a hard man in those days."

"What's he known as in these days?" Cate asked.

"Oh, he's a big shot. Inherited money, married money, president of a bank, lives in a mansion, socializes with the rich folks. Keeps up with society, don't you know," Rufus added with a mocking grin.

Cate left the newspaper office with the distinct impression that Rufus Bloy believed Fredrick Meyer had set fire to the McLaren house.

Chapter 8

Overnight the weather changed and the heat and humidity disappeared. The 4th of July was a perfect day with temperatures in the 70's and a slight breeze. Louis Pouline and Cate were enjoying their walk to the town center when the Gribbles saw them walking and stopped to pick them up. Emma and Nette's high spirits were contagious and Cate and Louis were laughing with the family as the driver maneuvered their buggy through the traffic jam converging on Red Jacket's main street. Cate wondered if every resident of the mining district was there. The streets were festooned with American flags and red, white and blue banners hung on buildings and across streets. Vendors hawking lemonade and root beer competed with the briskly patronized saloons.

Their driver stopped the buggy by the wooden sidewalk in front of the Emporium department store. As they stepped into the street, Cate expected a tight squeeze through the crowd but as soon as people saw the Gribbles they stepped aside with cheerful, "Good morning, Mr. Gribble, Mrs. Gribble."

Smiling, nodding, returning greetings, the Gribbles escorted their party up the Emporium steps to a raised, roped off platform where they joined the owners, Mr. & Mrs. Finlayson and their family.

Soon the street emptied of traffic and the Red Jacket City Band came marching down the street playing a stirring rendition of "Hail Columbia". They were followed by carriages containing members of the town council, the mayor, the day's speakers and the Grand Marshal. Then came the Light Infantry, looking smart in their new blue uniforms, more bands, marching groups, clowns, floats, and a fire company proudly displaying its new steam-powered fire truck. The grand finale was the proudly marching Civil War veterans.

The crowd cheered the veterans, applauded the bands, and laughed at the clowns. Boys ran alongside of the parade tossing firecrackers, then darting into the crowd to escape the marchers' anger. The supply of firecrackers seemed endless.

Opposite the Finlayson's Department Store stood the speakers stand. When the long parade ended the Rev. Heikkinen of the Apostolic Lutheran Church prayed for the safety of the Republic and the sobriety of its people. Some grumbling and hooting could be heard from the saloon element but most of the crowd, drinkers or not, thought the prayer eminently suitable. J. T. Asbury, professor of Mineralogy at the new College of Mines in nearby Houghton, stepped forward to read the Declaration of Independence.

Mrs. Gribble motioned to Cate and Louis to follow the family into the Emporium. As they headed for the backdoor and their waiting buggy, Mrs. Gribble explained, "We always leave right after the parade. This is a day for everyone to celebrate and the less we are around the more comfortable the workers will be."

"That is true, Miss Duncan," Mr. Gribble confirmed. "They are more comfortable when we are not around and so we leave early but still we consider this an extremely important day. It is one of the few days we close the mines so everyone can attend the festivities. The speeches can be entertaining and edifying, particularly for foreigners. Helps them learn the American way of thinking. One cannot expect immigrants to read English but most of the men and their families do learn to speak it. Then, for those who don't also learn to read, speeches like the one given today will teach them about the Declaration of Independence and the ideas and values that are important for our citizens. Educating people to become good citizens is very important. It is the reason the company builds schools and libraries."

July 5, 1885

Dear Mrs. Ogilve,

The 4th was a day of great celebration here. At the crack of dawn, yesterday, it seemed like every boy in town set off firecrackers and exploded tin cans. The main event of the day was a huge parade that began at 11 o'clock. It was exciting to be among thousands of people dressed in their best clothes cheering the bands and marching societies. Louis Pouline and I were with the Gribble family and we had a wonderful view of the parade on a raised platform in front of a department store.

The Gribble's picnic after the parade was an elegant affair. There were thirty-six of us, including the children, seated at four tables. The tables, laid with the finest linen, china, silver, and crystal, were placed under large shade trees.

That it was outside was the only way one could tell it was a picnic. Our first course consisted of platters of smoked lake trout, poached whitefish, roasted duck, and veal pies with sides of french peas, relishes, pickles, and sliced cucumbers. The second course offered roast beef, boiled beef, roast lamb, and ham. The sides were baskets of an excellent French salad, plates of tomatoes, and glasses of celery. Celery is a pleasant vegetable, mild tasting and crisp.

Mrs. Sincock says it is extremely expensive because it must be grown in a greenhouse. Mrs. Meyer, with her usual drop of superiority, let it be known that she'd frequently eaten celery in the best homes in Boston. Is Hulda serving celery at her dinner parties?

There was also a large variety of breads and rolls; for desert we had fresh fruits, cheeses, molded

puddings, blancmanges, jam puffs, pound cakes,
sponge cakes, strawberry shortcakes, and ice cream.

I was careful to take small portions, but,
even so, I felt like a stuffed turkey by the time we
finished. Fortunately, there were games for the
children and those of us still able to move after all
that food had a good time joining in.

Frederick Meyer was one of the guests. I
expected him to be cold and superior like his wife
but he was quite friendly and, much to my surprise,
I rather liked him. He obviously dotes on his seven-
year old son, Nathaniel. Nette and Nathaniel
seemed to be good friends and that speaks well for
the boy.

Mr. Meyer has asked me to give Nathaniel
piano lessons. I'm to meet with Mrs. Meyer
tomorrow to arrange a schedule. It feels a bit like
I'm being invited into the lion's den.

> *With Great Affection,*
> *Catherine*

As Cate addressed the envelope she
wondered what Mrs. Ogilve would think of the
'picnic' menu. And what would she have
thought had she known that when Cate took
her seat at the table the butler poured wine in
her glass.

When Louis Pouline saw Cate staring at
the wine as if it would bite her, he asked, "Is
something wrong with your wine?" Taking a
sip of his own, he added, "Mine is excellent."

"I'm sure mine must be also, but I don't
drink wine," Cate replied.

"Well, now is an excellent time to begin," he suggested. "This light French wine is perfect for a picnic. Why not take a small sip just to taste it?"

"No," she protested. "No, I couldn't do that,"

"Really," Louis raised one black eyebrow in puzzlement. "Why ever not?"

"I was raised by a Presbyterian minister and his wife," Cate explained.

"And what does that have to do with wine?" he asked.

"You don't know many Presbyterians, do you?" Cate replied, laughing. "We do not believe in drinking alcohol."

"Never?" he asked.

"Never," Cate said, shaking her head in emphasis.

"Well, I can certainly see why I haven't met many Presbyterians," Louis responded. "I'm sure they must have been outlawed in New Orleans.

"Well, now, if you are going to continue in society without drinking wine you will have to learn the signal that means not to fill your glass. As soon as you are seated at the dinner table turn over your wine glass. Then, whoever is pouring the wine will know that you do not want any."

Cate looked at Louis.

"Yes?" he inquired.

"Surely, you don't mean that I am to turn the glass upside down?" she asked, suspecting he was making fun of her.

"But I do," Louis responded laughing. "And you should." Leaning forward and looking across Cate to the gentleman seated on her right, Louis said, "Mr. Meyer, if a young woman does not wish to be served wine at a dinner party how should she handle it?"

"Handle it?" Fredrick Meyer asked, puzzled.

"Yes. How should she let the server know that she does not want her wine glass filled?" Louis explained.

"Oh, that's simple. Just turn the wine glass over. Takes care of it every time." Fredrick Meyer's voice was deep and pleasant. He smiled at Cate and asked, "Miss Duncan, are you the young lady who does not wish to be served wine?"

"Yes."

"Good for you," said Mr. Meyer, beaming at Cate and making her feel she had done something wonderful. "Nothing distinguishes a young lady more than good manners and temperance. Yes, indeed, good manners and temperance. Now mind you, for a married lady to have a glass of wine, well that's different, don't you see?"

Cate didn't see. But Fredrick Meyer had not really been asking her a question and he smoothly changed the subject asking flattering questions about her musical background.

Cate was not the first person to be charmed by Frederick Meyer. Charming people was a skill he had cultivated throughout his high-flying, and occasionally disastrous, business career. He had long ago learned that if people thought he was their friend, a good fellow with a hearty voice and beaming smile, they were more likely to give him the benefit of the doubt in times of trouble.

Not that he had to worry about that sort of thing anymore. No, inheriting his sister's Hecla mining stock and marrying Florence had changed things. He knew that people said he married Florence Payne for her money and that she married him because her family in Boston had sent her to Red Jacket because surely there, where men outnumbered women 20 to 1, she could find a husband.

He had always felt it was a great joke on the busybodies of the world that they were exactly right, those were the reasons they married. But what they didn't know was that there was more to it than that. Florence also brought the Payne name. A name so highly respected that all Fredrick had to do was drop it into the conversation and a hesitating stock purchaser was instantly reassured.

For people who wondered what she got out of the marriage, he knew the answer to that too. Respect. As a bone thin spinster over six feet tall she had too often endured stupid, unkind remarks. Now, wealthy in her own right and married to one of the leaders of the community, no one dared mock her.

The birth of Nathaniel Payne Meyer had solidified the marriage. He was their prince, their heir, their treasure. He seemed to have inherited the best features and qualities of both of them and, though they tried to spoil him, he remained a remarkably likable boy.

Because of Nathaniel, Fredrick had gotten out of the stock and insurance businesses where he was often tempted into risky, unethical ventures. Now, he stuck strictly to legitimate banking and took pride in the thought that one day Nate would take his place beside his father in the family bank.

Wednesday morning Cate stood in the front hall adjusting her hat in the mirror. The mirror reflected Mrs. Sincock hurrying towards her.

"Cate, I really wish you would take the buggy. You know I am not going out today so it will not matter when you come back."

Cate turned, smiling, "You are very kind, but I really prefer walking."

"Yes, yes, I know. You've always walked and you like to walk. But you lived in a very small town in a farming area. This not a small town and it is a mining area. We have hundreds of unmarried miners from all over the world. I'm not saying they are bad men, no, most of them are good men. But, some of them, once they start drinking, well... And you know that the taverns never close!" Exasperation and frustration were strong in her voice. This was not the first time she and Cate had discussed this, but she could see that Cate did not believe her.

"I'm just going to the Meyers to arrange Nate's lessons. There are no taverns on the way."

"No, there aren't. But what about when you go into town where there are taverns and men drinking all hours of the day and night?"

Cate sighed. "I can't very well avoid going into town. There are things I must do."

"You insist on walking?"

Cate nodded, "Yes."

"Then, at least, protect yourself." Mrs. Sincock triumphantly held out a long, strong hat pin.

"But, I already have a hat pin in my hat and more upstairs."

"This is not for your hat. It is for your purse! Yes, your purse. Keep it with you at all times. Then, anytime you are on the street alone just slip it into your hand."

Cate stared at the hat pin.

"Take it," she urged. "If nothing else, it will make me feel better."

"Perhaps you are right," Cate conceded, reaching for the pin. "Sometimes drunks do say things. I just keep on walking and I've been all right, but if someone did become troublesome and I had this in my hand I expect he would leave me alone. This is the biggest hat pin I've ever seen," Cate said, laughing.

Relieved and delighted Mrs. Sincock said, "You may be assured of that. My mother carried it and if the stories she told me were true it was very effective. This goes with it. It is a hollowed-out cork. Just slide the pin in and then it is safe to carry but easy to get at."

"But if this was your mother's I can't..."

"You can, and I insist."

"But what will you carry?"

She burst out laughing, "Heavens, at my age I don't need it. Besides, most of the men know I'm John Sincock's wife. If anyone bothered me the men who work for John would straighten him out before John even heard of it. I'm fine. You are the one who needs protection."

Cate nodded, opened her purse and dropped in the hat pin. "Thank you. I will carry this with me."

Watching Cate walk briskly down the street, Mrs. Sincock wondered if she had any idea what an attractive young woman she was and how that red hair made her stand out in any crowd. She sighed a bit remembering the days young men tried to catch her eye.

Cate walked out into a dark, windy, cold day. She shivered wondering how July could be so cold and was thoroughly chilled by the time she reached the Meyers. A long driveway led to the house. This is a mansion, Cate decided, a real one that made the Gribble home look ordinary. It was three stories high with huge white pillars reaching to the third-floor dominating the front of the house. A large covered porch swung around two sides of the ground floor, a smaller covered porch on the second-floor nestled between the huge pillars. Bay windows rounded the corners of the first and second floors. Windows were everywhere. In the front of the house Cate counted 18. At the far end of the driveway she could see a white carriage house that was a smaller version of the main house.

A maid answered the door. Cate was expected and as she was led to the music room she looked around with great curiosity knowing Mrs. Sincock would want a description of everything. The inside of the house was as impressive as the outside. In the center of the room size entrance hall there was a handsome carved oak staircase. The first room on the right was a richly decorated parlor sparkling from lamplight reflecting off a ceiling covered with silver leaves. The sitting room on the left was dominated by a mural covering one wall. Continuing down the hall Cate caught a glimpse of a large dining room decorated with stained glass windows.

When they reached the music room Cate was delighted to see a highly polished Steinway piano placed to take advantage of light from the windows. It was a fine piano.

Of course, she thought, Florence Meyer has only the best. Well, at least she takes proper care of her things. A sheet of music was open on the stand. Cate sat down and began to play it. It was the music from her dreams. Thrilled and terrified she played to the end.

She sat looking at her hands for a few moments and then, trembling, looked at the title. "*Morning Frolic*". The name did not mean anything to her. It was published by Schroeder & Schroeder, Philadelphia, Pennsylvania, 1865, composed by Susannah Meyer.

"I see you are looking at '*Morning Frolic*'," Florence Meyer said as she entered the room. Cate looked up startled. "Quite a nice little piece, isn't it? It was written by Mr. Meyer's sister. He is very proud of her work and insists that one of her compositions always be displayed on the piano."

"Are there more?" Cate asked eagerly.

"Oh, my, yes. Quite a number of her works were published. We have several of them. Unfortunately, neither Mr. Meyer nor I play the piano. I preferred the violin for my musical studies and Frederick simply was not interested as a child. However, he is eagerly looking forward to hearing Nathaniel play his sister's compositions.

"Which brings us to the point of your visit. I know that it is customary to receive one music lesson a week, but I understand that the Gribble girls are taking two and we will do the same. Morning would be the best time, preferably nine o'clock."

Lesson times were settled and Cate was dismissed. She walked to the Gribbles to give the girls their lessons in a daze, thinking, the grave stone said Susannah Meyer McLaren was my mother's name. The composer of *"Morning Frolic"*, the music from my dreams, is Susannah Meyer. Susannah Meyer is Fredrick Meyer's sister. If his sister married my father, becoming Susannah Meyer McLaren, then Fredrick Meyer is my uncle? Oh, surely not.

Chapter 9

Wednesday evening services over, Cate's friends gathered outside of the Presbyterian church laughing and talking. Normally, she joined them but tonight, still troubled by what she had learned at the Meyers, she wanted to be alone. When Maggie Loch called out to her to join the group, Cate smiled and waved but kept on walking.

"Miss Duncan!" Jamie called, hurrying after her. Reluctantly, she slowed down until Jamie caught up.

He smiled and apologized as they walked along. "I'm sorry to intrude but I've been wanting to speak with you ever since our visit to the cemetery; you seemed so upset afterwards. Is there anything I can do to help?"

Jamie glanced nervously at Cate as he spoke. He believed prying into other people's lives was wrong. Yet, his concern for Cate overcame that conviction, and here he was prying into the private life of a friend. A lovely friend, but just a friend.

Jamie knew that for the time being friendship was all there could be. He had no intention of being a laborer all of his life. No, he planned to own his own business one day and to do that he had to work hard and save every penny possible. The hard work had been rewarded in May when Mr. Charbonneau made him a foreman at the lumber yard. He knew he had the ability to make his dream come true but, until then, marriage was out of the question. No matter how strongly he was drawn to Cate Duncan he had no right to court her. Still, he could not deny when he saw her at the 4th of July parade, so tall and elegant in her white dress, her red hair gleaming under her straw hat, his heart had nearly stopped.

Cate was caught off guard by Jamie's concern. She had no intention of telling anyone in Red Jacket about her odd quest but so many doubts and fears had built up inside her that his care and concern disarmed her. Haltingly, she began to talk. Slowly they walked on past Sincock's house to a small park where they could talk in privacy.

Cate told Jamie about her childhood, the wonderful Ogilves who became her parents, her father's disappearance, Rev. Ogilve's death and the discovery of the briefcase. A case that contained a disturbing amount of money and odd financial papers, a photograph of Cate and her mother, and the still hard to digest news that her last name was not Duncan. She told him of Mrs. Ogilve encouraging her to travel to Red Jacket and discover the truth but that she did not expect the truth to be her own name and her father's name on the grave stones or

Rufus Bloy's suspicions that Fredrick Meyer murdered the family and burned down the house. She also told him of her joy when she discovered that the music of her memories, *Morning Frolic,* was composed by her mother and her delight that her mother had composed other pieces, as well. Finally, she spoke of her fear that Frederick Meyer was her uncle.

Jamie listened intently without interrupting. When Cate ended her story, he said, "I can see why you came to Red Jacket. But to come alone, not knowing anyone, that took courage and I think you have discovered a lot in a very short time."

"But everything I learn just makes it more confusing and I still have no idea why we left here or why my father changed my name," Cate pointed out.

"Not yet, you haven't," Jamie agreed, "but everything you've learned will help."

"How?" asked Cate.

"Well, look at what you found at the cemetery. There has to be something really wrong there. Why is there a tombstone with your name on it and one with your father's name? You are very much alive and from what the Ogilves said, your father was alive in August of 1870."

"I don't know." Cate shook her head in frustration. "I've thought and I've thought but I don't have any idea. And I've wondered, if I'm alive do you suppose my mother might be also?"

Jamie was quiet, thinking, then said, "You're right, she might be. It is a question that needs answering. Who is buried there?"

"How do we find out?" Cate asked.

"The undertaker who handled the burial should know. I think we need to find out who he was."

"Do you suppose he would still be here?" Cate asked.

"The caretaker at the cemetery might be able to tell us," Jamie suggested. "He has an excellent memory and loves to talk about the old days.

"I'll ask him. We may have a delivery this week, if not, Mr. Charbonneau has told me I may take a horse for private errands.

"If that is all right with you, Miss Duncan?" Jamie asked, suddenly realizing he was stepping into Cate's private life again.

"All right." Cate smiled and sighed with relief. "Yes. That is most definitely all right. And I think that as you know my whole life story you might just as well call me Cate."

"Cate," Jamie smiled as he gently spoke her name. "And I hope you will call me Jamie."

When Cate woke up Thursday morning Red Jacket seemed to shine with a special light. She laughed at herself knowing the light was not different from the day before. What was different was that now she had a friend in her quest and no longer felt so lonely and isolated.

Returning from morning lessons Cate checked the mail hoping to find a letter from

Mrs. Ogilve. Instead in the basket on the hall table was a letter from Dr. Weissmiller.

Quickly, she climbed the stairs to her room, entered and carefully closed the door. Taking a deep breath, she slowed down and deliberately removed her hat and gloves and put them away. She opened her lesson case and put away the lesson books. Then she picked up the envelope again and held it in her hand trying to decide if it was heavy enough to contain a contract. It felt too light. Carefully, she slit it open and extracted one sheet of paper.

Lincoln High School
Red Jacket
July 8, 1885

Miss Catherine Duncan
814 Hecla Ave., Red Jacket

Dear Miss Duncan:

It is my great pleasure to offer you a position as a teacher of elementary education with salary and schedule as discussed during our June meeting.

Please come to the office within the next week to sign your contract and receive your schedule of August teacher meetings.

Yours Truly,
Dr. Oscar Weissmiller

Elated, Cate danced around the room and then hurried downstairs calling, "Mrs. Sincock."

Freda answered, "She's out. Didn't say what time she'd be back."

"Oh ... thanks." Cate hesitated, then entered the living room and sat at the piano. Freda opened the kitchen door and secured it when she saw Cate go to the piano. Even when she was practicing a piece over and over Freda enjoyed listening.

But this was not a practice session. The music that erupted from the living room, wild and exuberant, came not from a piece of paper but from Cate. Something broke free and she let her own music flow from her fingers. She had no idea what she was playing, nor did she care. She just played, freely, thankfully, joyfully.

Chapter 10

Nate Meyer was Cate's first pupil who was taking lessons because he had to, not because he wanted to play the piano. Her pupils at Oberlin had all been eager students delighted to receive free lessons from a budding music teacher and the Gribble girls were well past the basics.

Nate did not know a half note from a quarter note, much less a sharp from a flat and it was obvious that he would rather play baseball than the piano. But he was a pleasant child and he paid attention to Cate's instructions. She liked Nate and looked forward to their lessons.

Nate had a tendency to be late for his lessons. In another student Cate would have found this annoying, but at the Meyers it gave her an opportunity to play her mother's compositions.

Florence Meyer, however, was annoyed with her son's tardiness. This was his sixth lesson and he had not been on time once. When Frederick and Nate returned from their morning fishing trip with full baskets and light hearts Florence sternly informed them, "You are being extremely impolite! Miss Duncan has been here since nine o'clock! Do you think she has nothing to do but wait for you?"

Nate ran up the backstairs to wash up and change. Frederick, hearing Cate playing one of his sister's compositions, stood in the hall, listening quietly. Watching her play he thought she almost looked like Susannah sitting there. When the music ended he stepped into the room.

"Bravo. Well done. It is a joy to hear that piece played."

"Thank you." Cate was surprised to see Fredrick Meyer standing there. "It is a lovely composition. Please do come in."

"Another time. Another time I will. At the moment I must get out of these fishing clothes. Mrs. Meyer tells me you have a fascination with my sister's music. Is that true?"

"Yes, I suppose I do." Cate flushed slightly, surprised at how tense the question made her feel.

"You know, it is odd that you like her music so much and that you actually look a bit like my sister. I expect it is just that she was tall and had red hair too. You don't happen to have any Meyer in your family, do you."

"No."

"Still, it's odd. Tell me, what was your mother's maiden name?"

"My, my mother's maiden name?" Cate stammered searching for a name. "Ah, well, yes. It was, ah, Ogilve."

As Cate hesitated, then blurted out, "Ogilve" Frederick Meyer realized she was uncomfortable with his questions. He watched the obvious relief on her face when Nate dashed into the room for his lesson. Slowly, Fredrick walked to the front hall and up the winding staircase to his room to change.

How very odd, he thought. How very odd, indeed. Why would a simple question about her mother's name cause such a reaction? I think it is time I find out about this young lady. Yes, I will ask Oscar Weissmiller about our new music teacher. When we approved hiring Miss Duncan at the school board meeting Oscar said she came well recommended from Oberlin. But what of her background, her family? Where is her home? And, though he tried to push it away to the back of his mind, the thought hovered that Catherine McLaren who could play the piano when she was 4 years old would be 20 today.

Saturday evening Jamie rushed home to wash and change and then hurried to the Sincock's worrying about what Cate must be thinking. He was almost two hours late for their five o'clock meeting.

When Cate answered the door Jamie burst out, "I'm sorry I'm so late."

He looked so uneasy that Cate could not help but smile, "I *was* beginning to worry that perhaps something had happened to you."

"No, I'm fine," he reassured her. "It's the schedule that was broken. Mr. Charbonneau planned to close early today but we received two large rush orders around one o'clock and ended up working until after six. That's why I'm so late and I do apologize but you needn't worry, I won't take up much of your time."

Puzzled, Cate asked, "Do you have another appointment?"

"No. But, I don't want to interfere with your plans for this evening."

Cate laughed. "My plans for this evening are to write letters and that is something I can do almost any evening. Please don't feel you must rush away on my account. And don't worry about the time, this is actually better because Mrs. Sincock sits down to supper promptly at 5:30 on Saturdays. Now, we can take all the time we need. Let's go and sit on the side porch."

Greatly relieved Cate was not angry with him, Jamie sat down and put his straw hat on the wicker table. "I wrote to you asking for this meeting because I've spoken to the cemetery caretaker, Mr. Prideaux. He said the cemetery does not keep records of which undertakers did which burials but he thinks it would have been Gregory's Funeral Home. He said Gregory's has been in business since the

1860's and it did most of the Protestant funerals in those days, particularly the upper-class ones."

Cate stood up. "I'm going to get a pencil and paper so that I can write down the name before I forget it. I'll be back in a minute," and with a quick smile she was gone.

It was more than a minute before Cate returned carrying a tray with a pitcher of lemonade, two chicken sandwiches, a plate of sugar cookies, glasses, and napkins.

"You must be hungry for you surely did not have time to eat before you arrived here. I made these sandwiches so you don't expire from hunger while we talk. And there is something I want to show you which may take awhile to discuss."

With a big grin and heartfelt, "Thank you!" Jamie reached for a sandwich. It had been a long time since lunch.

Cate returned to the house to fetch her father's briefcase.

"This briefcase changed my life." Carefully, she snapped opened the locks. "Everything is in it as it was when I first opened it except for the money that I put in the bank and this photo that I keep in my room." Cate handed the photo in its silver frame to Jamie.

"You look like your mother," Jamie commented. "It is a strong resemblance."

"I'm glad you think so," Cate replied, obviously pleased. "Mrs. Ogilve thought so too, and I must admit after wondering about my parents for so many years to find a photograph of them and see that my mother and I look alike--it was almost overwhelming."

Turning back to the briefcase, Cate said, "You can see that everything was neatly packed. This packet has boat and train tickets and hotel reservations for Detroit, Buffalo, New York and London."

Jamie looked them over. "Those are famous hotels that your parents were going stay in. They must have been very well-to-do."

"They were," Cate agreed handing him her parents bank statements.

His eyes widened, "Indeed they were. Do you know what happened to all this money?"

"No. But, Rufus Bloy said Fredrick Meyer inherited everything. I suppose he got it. Now, this packet seems to do with business," Cate explained. "It is a small ledger and letters."

Jamie examined the ledger. There were pages of names, dates, and dollar amounts with question marks after some names. "It appears to be records of payments in and out. Do you know if these are saving accounts?"

"No. That is why I decided to show it to you. I have no business experience and no idea what this means."

Jamie picked up a packet of letters. He glanced through them, then picked up the ledger again and began comparing letter names and ledger names.

"These are letters to The German & Slovenian Miners Bank written in foreign languages."

"Yes," Cate agreed, "that much I could figure out. Unfortunately they are not French or German, the only foreign languages I know."

"Ah," Jamie paused and sighed. "You have a fine education." He turned his attention back to the letters. "The postmarks on the envelops come from Poland, Finland and Hungry. I can't read them but look, some of the names on the envelopes are similar to names in the ledger." Jamie picked up another a large envelope. That had "COPIES" written across it. "These are copies of letters from the bank. Let's see if there are any name matches."

"Some of these names do look the same," Cate said as they carefully compared them. "If only we knew what they said!"

"You could have them translated," Jamie suggested. "There are men from Finland and Poland working at the lumber yard. I could ask them."

"That's a good idea," Cate agreed. "Do you think they could keep what the letters said confidential?"

Jamie laughed, "That I don't know. But if you want it keep confidential maybe we should ask Rev. Campbell. He knows which ministers and priests preach in foreign languages and which ones are reliable."

Cate agreed and suggested they pick letters to be translated from names checked in the ledger which had written to the bank and had a letter from the bank in the copy file.

Monday morning Cate called on Rev. Campbell seeking translators who would keep the contents of the letters confidential. Happy to oblige he suggested, Father Pawler, St. Anthony's Catholic Church, Reverend Heimonen, The Finnish Lutheran Church and Father Karinen at St. Joseph's Catholic Church. He also offered to write letters of introduction for Cate. Thanking him wholeheartedly she left to give Nate Meyer his music lesson. As she walked along Cate also thanked God for bringing such a good, kind man into her life.

That afternoon Cate picked up the letters and began her translation quest. The churches were widely separated and walking from one church to another took most of the afternoon. Enjoying the lovely day she looked around with great interest as she walked through unfamiliar neighborhoods. Here were company houses, two-story, four-bedroom, unpainted wooden homes on large lots built close to the sidewalks. Flowers and small patches of grass lined front yards while many of the back yards were given over to large vegetable gardens.

Cate was particularly interested in the children, wondering which ones would be her pupils. She noted with some relief that most of the children spoke English to each other even while the adults around them spoke a foreign language.

Passing a baseball field, she smiled seeing Nate Meyer playing third base and wondered if his mother knew he played with miner's children? Knowing Florence Meyer would not approve of such a thing, Cate decided Nate would not burden his mother with such information.

Cate went on her way humming the melody of "I'm Captain Jinks of The Horse Marines" and making up her own lyrics beginning with, "I'm Captain Nate of the Baseball Team."

When she reached the churches, Cate found Rev. Campbell's letters of introduction smoothed her way. She was given an opportunity to explain that she needed a translator for letters that were 15 or more years old, that she believed they were business letters, and that they must be kept confidential because they might contain information damaging to individuals presently living in Red Jacket.

Father Pawler and Reverend Heimonen agreed to translate the Polish and Finnish letters and assured her that confidentiality was part of their daily life. They did add that they could not be sure when they would finish the translations as they would have to fit the work into their busy schedules. Father Karinen said the letters from Hungry were written in Slovenian. He could not translate them but he knew a reliable person who could.

Cate should have felt tired as she hurried home for dinner having walked from one end of town to the other but she was so pleased with the day's work that she felt invigorated and optimistic. Tomorrow she would visit Mr. Gregory at Gregory's Funeral Home. It would be interesting to hear him explain how she and her father were, and were not, buried in the cemetery.   A   wild, three-day thunder, lightning, wind, and rainstorm changed Cate's plan. She struggled through the wind and rain to music lessons but did not attempt to go to Gregory's. Instead she spent the time laying out lesson plans for her school classes and practicing Mozart's "Sonata in A Minor". The Musical Society was to present a program at Hancock, a nearby business town on Portage Lake. Cate had been asked to accompany Emma and Jim Wright and to perform herself. She was eager to make a good impression. It wouldn't do, she thought to have the new music teacher stumble through her piece.

Friday broke with the sun rising into a clear blue sky. How bright and green and beautiful everything looked after the dark days of rain. With high hopes Cate set out to meet Mr. Gregory, but they did not last when she learned that old Mr. Gregory, who had been the mortician in 1870, had died and the present

Mr. Gregory had been a ten-year-old child at that time.

Cate's spirits were not raised by the letter awaiting her return home.

Thursday July 20,
Chicago, Illinois

Dear Catherine,

I have received disquieting news. Isobel Butler writes that on Tuesday of this week, a Mr. Black was in Grand Falls making inquiries about you. He knocked on her door claiming he represented the Fidelity Insurance Company and that, because you were buying a very large insurance policy, the company was checking on your character and financial situation.

Isobel thought it highly unlikely that you would be buying an insurance policy of any kind. Then, when his questions were all about when and why you came to live with us, she sent him on his way. He then went all over town, asking about you.

Isobel was so troubled by the incident that she wrote to me. I also find it disturbing. Be careful as you investigate what happened in 1870. You may want to consider letting the mystery remain unsolved for your own safety. Your father did not strike me as an easily frightened man, but something drove him away from his home and caused him to change your name.

Affectionately,
Harriet Ogilve

P.S. Isobel describes Mr. Black as about 5 foot 8 inches tall, quite stocky, with slightly graying, brown hair, receding on the temples. He was very well dressed, or as Isobel put it, "expensively dressed" and seemed to suffer from the heat and humidity.

Cate set the letter on her dresser and thought about Wednesday morning. She had finished the music lesson and was just leaving when she overheard Florence Meyer say to Nate, "I've a letter from your father. He will be home on the evening train."

"Yea!" said Nate happily.

"I think those will be your father's sentiments, exactly." Florence smiled. "He says the heat and humidity in Chicago have been almost unbearable."

Chicago? Cate wondered. Or maybe, Chicago and Great Falls.

Chapter 11

Cate struggled to concentrate on *A Brief Course in Education Theory*. The Sincock's grandfather clock struck eight. She sighed and closed the book. She was sure it must be edifying if she could only get past the mind-numbing sentences. And why, she wondered, hadn't she accepted Pearl and Opal's invitation to go with them to the park and enjoy the Cornet Band concert. It was silly staying home on a Friday night, even the Sincock's were visiting friends.

Cate went to the front of the porch and sat on the swing. She stopped swinging and leaned forward trying to see if it was Jamie coming down the street? It was. Quickly, she leaned back into the swing and began watching a nonexistent bird on a nearby tree.

Jamie turned up the walk and Cate rose to meet him.

"Hello," she called out. "Are you coming to see me?"

He laughed, "Well, I just happened to be walking by and I noticed you on the porch. It didn't seem polite not to stop and say hello."

"You are quite right. It would have been most impolite."

"And then I thought, well, I'm on my way to the Cornet Band concert, perhaps you might enjoy hearing it, too."

"I would very much enjoy going to the concert. Just give me a minute to get my hat."

Jamie and Cate were late arriving at the park. The band was already playing and all of the good seats were taken. As they looked around for seats, Cate was embarrassed when the Yeo twins caught her eye and looked at her as if to say, "Ho, ho, ho. So that's why you wouldn't come with us." Finally, Jamie found a spot where they could sit and enjoy the music and watch a glorious setting sun.

When the concert was over they walked slowly home in a soft velvet darkness. "What do you think of the Cornet Band?" Jamie asked.

"They are very good," said Cate. "I must admit I'd never heard of a cornet band before and wondered a bit, but they are excellent musicians. Their waltz selections were wonderful."

"A pity we could not have danced as well as listened," said Jamie.

"I don't know how to waltz," Cate admitted.

"It's not difficult," he assured her. "It's as easy to learn as any other dance."

"But I don't know any other dances either. I've never even been to a dance."

"But you're a musician." Jamie was stunned. "You play the organ, the piano."

"Yes, I know. But we just did not have dances in Great Falls or at Oberlin and I don't remember the Ogilves ever even talking about dancing." Taking a deep breath, Cate added, "I don't know how to ride a horse or drive a buggy either. It was too expensive for Rev. Ogilve to keep a horse in a town so small that we could walk everywhere. I never thought about it until moving to Red Jacket. There are so many people and everything is spread out here and so far apart--it would be nice to be able to drive instead of walk sometimes."

"I could teach you, if you are interested," Jamie offered.

"To drive?" Cate asked.

"Well," Jamie laughed. "Yes. To drive a horse and buggy, and to waltz too, if you wish."

"It seems a lot to ask you to do both, but..."

"But?"

"I do want to learn to drive a buggy and," Cate hesitated, "the Gribbles are having an anniversary party in August. Nette says her parents are hiring a boat that runs moonlight dance cruises along the Portage Lake Canal. Nette is excited about it because she and Emma will be at the party. She said my name is on the guest list and keeps asking me to promise I'll come.

"Mrs. Gribble has been so supportive of me that it would be difficult to decline an invitation from her. But to accept not knowing how to dance seems wrong too."

"Then you must learn to dance, at least enough to enjoy the evening."

"Yes, I suppose so. But, Nette might be wrong about the invitation and I'd rather learn to drive a buggy."

They turned up the Sincock's walk and stopped at the foot of the porch steps. Cate tuned to Jamie.

"Thank you for rescuing me this evening. It was a wonderful concert."

Jamie removed his hat, shook Cate's hand, and said, "It was. And thank you for accompanying me. Good night."

Halfway down the walk Jamie turned around, "Would Sunday afternoon be a good time for a driving lesson?"

"Oh, yes," said Cate. "It would be an excellent time."

"That's when it will be then," said Jamie, and with a tip of his hat he left.

Monday afternoon Cate walked briskly home from a meeting of elementary school principals and music teachers. The oppressive midday heat was gone and a lovely cool breeze promised a fine evening. As the first day of school drew closer she was beginning to feel nervous and excited but it helped to have met her coworkers and found out how helpful and encouraging they were. Now, she thought, if I can just remember their names.

Barking and snarling, a huge black dog charged at Cate. Startled, she leaped backward just as the dog, reaching the end of his chain, flipped in the air and landed just short of the sidewalk. Shaken and furious Cate ran past his ferocious barking.

She arrived home fuming. "Someday, someone is going to kill that dog and good luck to them."

Mrs. Sincock tried to look sympathetic but a small smile played about her lips. "Forgot about the brute, did you?"

"Yes! And I do think someone ought to talk to Mr. Thiele."

"Ah, that would do no good. Believe me, it's been tried. Nasty old man just sneers and says Blackie's doing just what he is supposed to do, protect the property and keep pests off of his land. Then he'll say, 'And if someone don't like the dog then they could bloody well walk on the other side of the street.' There is no moving that man."

Cate sighed, "I know, you told me about the dog when I moved in and I have walked on the other side of the street, until today, but it is just so annoying!"

She nodded agreement, then hoping to cheer Cate up, said, "There is a big package on the hall table for you. Now, Mr. Sincock will not be home to supper tonight and we are just having chicken casserole, corn on the cob and fresh tomatoes. The casserole will keep and I'll wait to put the corn on until you come down. So take your time washing up and go ahead and open your package."

It was from Rev Elo Heimonen, Finnish Lutheran Church, 608 Garnet Street, Red Jacket, Michigan. Cate hurried up to her room and quickly put away her hat, gloves, and school material. Then seating herself by the open window she carefully slit open the package and removed the letters she had given Rev. Heimonen. The first translated letter was to The German and Slovenian Bank.

February 22, 1868

Gentlemen:

In November a letter came from The Hecla Mining Company to tell me my husband, Carl Lehti, was dead in the mine. They sent me his pay and $50 death benefit.

From then I wait for you to send me the insurance money that Carl wrote that he had with the GENERAL TRUST Life Insurance Company. He wrote that he was paying every week for that insurance and that never would he miss a payment even if it meant going without because he said that was all there would be to support us if he got killed in the mine like he did.

Maybe you don't know my address. Here I write it so you can send me the money which I need to feed my children.

> *Turfmound Road*
> *Oulu, Finland*
> *Lina Lehti*

Pres., F. M. Meyer
Sec.Treas., A. D. Mclaren
OFFICE OF GERMAN & SLOVENIAN
MINERS BANK
601 Laurium Street
Red Jacket, Michigan

March 22, 1868

Mrs. Carl Lehti
Turfmound Road
Oulu, Finland

Madam:

Please accept our condolences on the tragic death of your husband Carl Lehti.

With regard to his insurance policy: we regret to inform you that THE GENERAL TRUST Insurance Company denied payment because Carl signed up as an above ground worker. The GENERAL TRUST policy clearly states they do not insure miners. Carl's death in underground mining accident negated his policy.

We explained to General Insurance that this tragedy must have occurred because of Carl's lack of English and prevailed upon them to return his premium payments of $30. Because we are deeply troubled by this matter we are adding to that $70 of our own money. While this is not the $1,000 dollars you expected we trust it will be of some help.

Enclosed find a bill of transfer for $100.

Sincerely Yours,
Alexander McLaren

July 10, 1869

Gentlemen,

News has come that my brother Jacob Kolehmainen died while visiting friends in Detroit, Michigan, May 6. He was buried in the Swedish Lutheran Church Cemetery there. With this letter I send you the letter from Pastor Gundsweld telling of Jacob's death and burial so you know what I say is true. Jacob wrote to me that he had insurance with you and if he should die I am to get one thousand dollars. Please send the money to my address. Also, please send back the letter from Pastor Gundsweld as it means much to me.

Matta Kolehmainen
4 Vaasa
Kotka, Finland

Pres., F. M. Meyer
Sec.Treas., A. D. Mclaren
OFFICE OF GERMAN & SLOVENIAN
MINERS BANK
601 Laurium Street
Red Jacket, Michigan

Sept. 6, 1869

Miss Matta Kolehmainen
4 Vaasa
Kotka, Finland

Dear Miss Kolehmainen,
It is with regret that we inform you that, while Jacob Kolehmainen did at one time have a life

insurance policy with us, he stopped making payments on that policy and it had lapsed at the time of his death.

We can only offer you our heartfelt condolences at your tragic loss. Your letter from Pastor Gundsweld is enclosed.

Respectfully,
Alexander McLaren

The last letter was from Pastor Heimonen.

Dear Miss Duncan,

I am often called upon to write letters in Finnish or to translate letters from Finnish. Through this activity I have become exposed to and educated in handwriting and signatures. Perhaps it is of no importance but as you are concerned about the contents of the letters I thought you might be interested in knowing that the letters from Alexander McLaren appear to be signed by two different people.

It may mean nothing, of course, but on the off chance that it might be important I felt you should know.

Please do not hesitate to call on me if I can be of further use.

Sincerely Yours,
Elo Heimonen

Cate carefully examined the signatures on the letters. She had not noticed it when she first saw them but they did look somewhat different. I wonder what Jamie would think of them. Should I write and ask him to visit? No, not yet. I can't keep bothering him every two days. I'll wait until another set of letters arrives.

Later that evening Cate did write to Mrs. Ogilve.

Monday, Aug. 9.

Dear Mrs. Ogilve,

Would you believe that I am learning to drive a horse and buggy?

My instructor is James Dunn, the young man who rescued me from the irate bear at the church picnic. We have become friends and when I told him I did not know how to drive, he offered to teach me.

Sunday, after church we went to the countryside for my first lesson. I was surprised to discover that my lesson began with me standing next to the buggy.

I had to learn how to take the reins from the buggy and, by keeping just the right pressure on the horse's mouth, keep him from moving while I climb up onto the buggy seat. Holding the reins properly and maintaining the correct pressure on the horse's mouth is very important to prevent the horse from getting the bit in its teeth and running away.

The first time I signaled the horse to move forward it felt like we were flying through the air and he was just walking! Walking the horse I learned how to turn and to stop. I was feeling rather proud of myself, but I should have remembered what goes before a fall because when we began trotting I did everything wrong! First I held the reins too loosely and the horse went too fast and then I pulled too hard on the reins and she jerked to a stop. The poor horse lost patience then tossing her head and snorting to let me know what she thought of my driving.

I'm afraid for my first lesson I was all awkward thumbs, but I am so delighted with driving that I can hardly wait for next Sunday and another lesson.

On our way home, I told Mr. Dunn I hope when I am teaching I will remember how difficult it is to learn new things.

Last week I received 10 of my mother's compositions from her publisher, Schroeder & Schroeder. These are not the only ones they published but they are the only titles they have left in stock. Of course, I would like to have everything my mother wrote but I am so delighted to have these that I've neglected almost everything else to play them. There are three in particular I think are outstanding and I have ordered them for you. Do let me know what you think of them.

Friday is fast approaching. That is the night of the musical at Meyers. The performance was moved from the home in Hancock to Meyers because so many people wished to attend. Mr. & Mrs. Sincock have been invited and Mrs. Sincock is delighted to be included and eager to see the inside of the Meyer mansion.

I am happy for her but wish we were playing somewhere else. I told you how strange it is to give lessons to my cousin and say nothing about our relationship. It helps immensely that Nate and I get along so well. That has not happened with Mr.

Meyer. He has changed from friendly to cold since he returned from the trip to Grand Falls.

He must know who I am. Why else would he be asking questions about me? Do you think he is afraid I will try and prove who I am and then he would have to give me the money he inherited from my mother? I do not want the money!

With Great Affection,
Catherine

Chapter 12

"Now you're sure we can't give you a ride home?" James Wright asked Cate as he ushered Sally Hutchinson out the door.

"No. Thank you very much for the offer but it is only a few blocks and I do enjoy walking," Cate said, maintaining a very straight face. The minute the door closed she and Erma burst out laughing.

"I do believe he would have had apoplexy if you'd accepted his offer," Erma said, shaking her head. "I have never seen James so gaga over any girl. Do you suppose she is going to capture him?"

"It rather looks like it," Cate answered. "It's a pity she can't even carry a tune though."

"Don't worry about that. James will sing enough for both of them. To tell the truth, he was not too thrilled when I began singing too," Erma confided as she opened the door for Cate.

Cate was surprised to step out into the gathering dark. Their rehearsal had lasted longer than normal but she had not realized it was this late. The afterglow of the setting sun was gone and shadows were rapidly disappearing into blackness. The heavy sound of machinery, trains, and shrill steam whistles from the copper mines traveled through the night air making an odd contrast to the quiet residential streets.

Uneasy, Cate pulled out Mrs. Sincock's huge hat pin and placed the ball end securely in the palm of her hand. She had to admit it made her feel better and made a mental note to thank her for insisting she take it.

Turning a corner, Cate glanced back. The street was empty. She realized she had been glancing back a lot the last few days, feeling someone was looking at her, or following her. Here I am doing it again and there never is anyone there. It's just my imagination, she decided, and determined to be sensible, moved briskly along.

Half a block later she felt it again. Someone was staring at her. Walking as fast as she could she kept looking back but it was too dark to see far and she was afraid to stop and look. Whoever it was might catch up if she slowed down.

Cate gasped when the man stepped out from a hedge and blocked her way. Huge, calloused hands grabbed her upper arms and jerked her towards him. The strong fumes of alcohol and unwashed clothes enveloped Cate.

"Kind of in a hurry ain't you Miss Snooping Rich Bitch?" he mocked.

Terror's adrenaline gave Cate great strength as she slammed the heavy hat pin upwards through his shirt sleeve, through the skin, stabbing into the bone. The man screamed and jerked away. Terrified, Cate ran.

She could hear him pounding after her, his curses and threats becoming clearer as he came closer. Gasping and stumbling she turned the corner on to Hecla Street. Please, oh please, somebody be out she shouted silently. But no one was out. The street stretched before her dark, empty.

Cate ran on, but he was getting closer. Oh, please be out. Please, she prayed.

Barking and snarling, Blackie charged. Cate flew past hoping the dog would startle and slow the man. There was a loud snap as Blackie's chain broke and suddenly the man was kicking and yelling as the dog, finally free to attack, went after him. Dog and man became a rolling, cursing, snarling ball.

Cate kept running until she was inside the Sincock's house. Collapsing against the front door she locked it and leaned trembling against it. Her heart was pounding so hard she looked at her chest almost expecting to see it beating out. Sweat ran into her eyes and down her arms and legs.

Warily, she looked out of the glass panels on the front door. She stood a long time watching. If he had followed her home she could not see him. Cate put out the light Mrs. Sincock had left burning for her and moved to the back of the house to be sure the backdoor was locked.

Slowly, Cate climbed the back stairs. When she entered her room she locked the door. She did not light her lamp. If he was out there she was not going to let him know which was her room. She stood near the front window looking out for several minutes, then moved to the side window and did the same. All was quiet.

Cate was exhausted. She walked into the closet and peeled off her sweaty clothes, dropping them on the floor. I should hang them up she thought as she walked to her bed. Pulling out the pins that held her hair in place she put them on the bed table and crawled into bed, naked. Never in her life had she done such a thing, but right now she was too hot, too sore, too scared, and too tired to care.

Chapter 13

Bam, bam, bam. Cate woke up. Someone was pounding on her bedroom door.

"Cate! Cate! Are you all right?" Mrs. Sincock yelled through the locked door.

Groggily, Cate answered. "Yes. Yes, I'm fine."

The knocking stopped and there was a long silence. "I was worried about you," Mrs. Sincock explained. "You are usually up at 6 o'clock and it is almost eight! If you do not get up soon you won't have time to eat breakfast before you must leave to give your lessons. Are you sure you're not ill? It would be such a shame if you had to miss the musical tonight after all of the time you spent practicing."

"Yes. No. I mean I'm fine. And thank you for waking me. I'll get right up."

Still half asleep, Cate lay in bed thinking how bright and colorful the room looked with the sun shining in on the striped white and pink wallpaper. Lazily, her eyes followed the wallpaper border of small pink roses and green leaves, then dropped to the gold and white dressing table and the dark blue rugs scattered on the floor. She was surprised to see the closet door wide open. Finally Cate got out of bed. She stood still, astonished to discover she was naked. And then she remembered why the closet door was open.

Feeling defenseless and exposed without clothes, Cate dressed quickly. As she brushed out the tangles in her hair she debated what to tell Mrs. Sincock about the night before. Nothing. I will say nothing because if do tell about the drunk she will try to prevent me from walking anywhere by myself.

I suppose I really should not walk alone at night anymore. Thank heavens I don't have to worry about walking in the daytime. Even a drunk won't molest a respectable woman in daylight.

Cate hurried down to breakfast relieved that she would not have to tell Mrs. Sincock about the man who grabbed her but a little sorry that she couldn't tell her that the horrible dog, Blackie, had actually been her savior.

The morning mail brought a letter from Louis Pouline.

Aug. 14

Dear Miss Duncan,

I would consider is a great honor if you would permit me to escort you to the Meyers this evening. If this is agreeable to you, I will come for you at 7:30.

Sincerely,
Louis Pouline

Thoughtfully, Cate set the note on her desk. She had enjoyed the Fourth of July with Louis at the Gribbles, but he had hardly spoken to her since then, even when they were at the same social events. So what precipitated this letter? Well, there was only one way to find out.

She picked up her pen and wrote an acceptance note.

At 7:30 that evening, Cate was struggling to put up her hair but the long red curls refused to cooperate.

Freda appeared at the bedroom door to tell Cate that Mr. Pouline had arrived. Seeing Cate's frustration she entered the room saying, "Here, let me help you. And don't you worry about Mr. Pouline waiting, Mrs. Sincock is entertaining him in the front parlor. Now, just relax and let me fix your hair."

"Are you sure you are not a magician?" Cate asked, watching Freda's expert fingers fly.

Freda laughed, "I'm no magician and I'm not nervous either."

Cate smiled. "Your right, I am nervous."

"Now, stand up and turn around," Freda commanded. Carefully she looked over Cate's silk dress from the fit of the cream-colored bodice to the drape of the brown and gold stripped skirt. She nodded her head and smiled. "You'll do."

With grateful thanks to Freda, Cate hurried downstairs. Louis and Mrs. Sincock were laughing together in the front parlor and from the delighted sparkle in Anna's eyes Cate was sure Louis had claimed another admirer.

Cate's nerves did not calm down until she actually sat at the Meyer's piano and began playing Mozart's, "*Sonata In A Minor*". She was surprised and pleased when the burst of applause that erupted at the end of her piece went on and on. Finally, James Wright, who had taken charge of introducing the musicians, held up his hand to silence the applause. Turning to Cate he said, "I think this calls for an encore." A chorus of "Here, here" agreed with him.

Sitting on the piano bench, hands folded together above the keys, Cate thought for a moment, then said, "As a thank you to Mr. & Mrs. Meyer for so kindly hosting this Musicale, I will play, "*Morning Frolic*", which was composed by Mr. Meyer's sister, Susannah Meyer."

Florence smiled and nodded, graciously accepting the gift. Frederick looked neither pleased nor displeased but there was an anger in his eyes that chilled Cate. Her heart lighted when she saw Nate's huge grin as he and Nette sat forward in their seats eagerly waiting for her to begin.

"What a triumph you had this evening," Louis exclaimed as he drove Cate home.

It had been rather a triumph Cate knew and at first she had been delighted with the prolonged applause and the request for encores. But she was not prepared to deal with the verbal complements that continued throughout the evening and was thoroughly tried of the subject.

"I can't deny that I'm gratified that my playing was so well received but I do think people are excessively complimentary," Cate said hoping Louis would drop the subject.

"I noticed you were uncomfortable when anyone praised your playing tonight," Louis commented. "Don't you like compliments?"

"Not excessive ones."

"Ah, but they weren't excessive. People were just trying to tell you how much they enjoyed your playing."

Cate didn't respond, knowing anything she said would sound ungrateful.

"Maybe it's that small town you come from," Louis began.

"Small town?" Cate interrupted, wondering just when and where did I tell you anything about where I came from?

"Yes," Louis replied. "Grand Falls, only about 1,200 people, aren't there? A little farming town. No culture, really. Wasn't it one of those places where everyone was straight-laced? No drinking, no partying, no excessive compliments." Louis smiled at Cate with his most winning smile. "Am I wrong?"

"It was somewhat like that," Cate conceded, remembering she had told him about the attitude toward drinking.

"That's what intrigues me," he said. "How a talented, cultured person like you came from a small farming community? Surely your family weren't farmers?"

"Didn't I mention I was raised in a manse?"

"That's right you did. I suppose that explains it. Your family really wasn't from Grand Falls originally. Where did they come from?

"New England," said Cate in a most pleasant voice as she began to suspect that this conversation was the purpose of Mr. Pouline's wish to escort her. He was on a fishing expedition for his boss, Frederick Meyer, who had recently been in Grand Falls. A little farming town of 1,200 people was not something Cate ever said because she had had no idea how many people lived there.

"Yes, it was New England. I don't remember much talk about it. My father believed in paying attention to today. And my mother had some sort of problem with her family. A brother she didn't want to talk about. I'm not sure what the problem was but it was something dishonorable." Cate smiled sweetly as she wondered what Fredrick Meyer's reaction would be to that little bit of information. "Isn't it wonderful that you are interested in family history." She continued. "You must tell me all about your family. Where did they come from before New Orleans?" And Louis, ever happy to talk about himself, spent the rest of their ride telling her about his distinguished ancestors.

By the time she went to bed Cate had decided that she really wanted to be able to drive herself to evening events. It would be several weeks before she could do that with the once a week lessons but if she practiced in between, just like she did with the piano, she might be able to drive sooner. She'd start tomorrow, if the Sincocks were not using the buggy for an hour or so.

And it was time to contact Jamie and tell him about the insurance letters, the feeling of being followed, and the attack by the drunk. And Louis Pouline asking questions about where she came from. First thing in the morning, she would write and ask Jamie to come by after work.

Chapter 14

Cautiously encouraging Peggy forward, Cate maneuvered the Sincock's buggy onto the street. Tense, nervous, and fearful she would not be able to control the horse, Cate could hardly breathe as Peggy moved along at a brisk walk. Mrs. Sincock often complained it was almost impossible to get any speed out of her. Cate fervently hoped that was true. Even at a walk it was terrifying to guide Peggy around corners.

Carefully choosing the least traveled roads through the mining district Cate soon reached the countryside. Her journey did not seem so terrifying when there were no buggies to avoid or people crossing streets to worry about. She began to enjoy herself. She wasn't going to go far, only about five miles to the natural spring Jamie had shown her. It was in a small meadow alongside the forest road and there was lots of room to turn the buggy around.

Perhaps I'll look for wildflowers while I'm there Cate thought. Mrs. Sincock was talking about how beautiful they are the other day. I expect it would please her no end if I brought her a small bouquet. And I've time. Jamie won't be over until after 4. He said he had news for me too. I wonder what it is?

Cate drove on enjoying the meadows and the scattering of wildflowers. Dust swirled up behind the buggy and sweat began to bead on her forehead as the August sun beat down.

How nice it is to be out here and not worry about anybody following me or staring at me. I wonder if it is just being in town that makes me feel I'm being stared at, because even today, driving Peggy, I felt it? It wasn't until we were past the mines that it went away.

The straight, fairly smooth country road became rough and winding when it entered the forest. The easy part of the ride was over and Cate gripped the reins tightly. Stop pulling back so strongly or Peggy will stop, she told herself. Peggy knows what she's doing, just let her decide how to go.

The horse moved along at her comfortable pace and Cate, alternating tightening and loosening the reins bounced about on the buggy seat. She knew she must be doing something wrong because she had not bounced around when Jamie was driving. It was a relief to reach the spring and bring the buggy to a stop.

Shakily, Cate climbed down from the seat. She was surprised at how tired she felt.

"We both need a drink of water," Cate said, leading Peggy to the special horse's troth at the foot of the spring. Cate cupped her hands to catch the water bubbling out from the top of the rock. Jamie said it tasted so good because it came up through the copper underground. Cate had no idea if that was true but she had to admit it was wonderfully cold and refreshing.

Feeling her energy return, Cate tied Peggy to a tree limb and began to search for wildflowers.

It was Peggy whinnying that made Cate turn around. A chill ran down her back when she saw Fredrick Meyer leading his horse onto the small meadow. He was dressed for business in a black suit, gray vest, stiff, high collared white shirt, gray tie and a black bowler hat. He looked as cool and in control as if he sat in his office. He did not smile.

He said, "You are out here alone." It was a statement, not a question.

Cautiously, Cate moved towards her buggy. "I wanted to pick wildflowers." she explained nervously.

"Or perhaps you wanted to learn to drive a buggy. You certainly were not raised in a family who owned one," his voice mocked her.

Cate moved to Peggy. Flustered, she fumbled with the reins, trying to untie them from the tree.

"You really should know better than to go out into the countryside alone," Meyer said, moving towards her. "Don't you know what can happen to girls who wander away? Terrible things can happen." He tied his horse to the back of the Sincock's buggy.

Cate finally freed the reins from the branch and began to climb into the buggy. Meyer grabbed her arm, yanked the reins away and shoved her ahead of him onto the buggy seat. She tried to jerk away, struggling to free herself, but Meyer's grip was like an iron vise. With one hand for Cate and the other for the reins, he skillfully turned Peggy out of the meadow, heading away from Red Jacket.

"Some get lost in the forest," Meyer continued once they were moving, "and are never found. A difficult way to die don't you think? Some are attacked by drunks and found by the side of the road." He glanced at Cate as he added, "Just like what should have happened to a foolish girl who walked alone at night." Cate's heart sank but she said nothing so Myers continued his monolog. "And a few ... just disappear.

"One never knows if they ran away or ..." he paused and then said angrily, "One can say that they all were stupid. And you, my dear niece, are the stupidest of all!

"You did not get that from your mother. She was brilliant. No, you definitely take after your father."

Cate finally found her tongue. "If you thought she was so brilliant why did you kill her?"

"Kill her? Who has been filling your head with such nonsense. Not your fool of a father. He knew who killed her but he would have been much too much the honorable Christian to have told a five-year-old. Who says I killed her?" he demanded.

"You did it. You did it for the money," Cate challenged.

"No. No, you little fool, I loved my sister. Besides, eventually she would have given me the money anyway to save her sainted husband." Fredrick laughed triumphantly.

"What do mean? Why would she have given you her money?"

"To save her husband who had been fleecing dumb immigrants by taking their money for insurance policies and putting it in his own pocket, or sending in the payments and then, when they died, keeping the death benefit for himself instead of sending it to the family. If letters came asking for payment they'd be told the insurance policy was no good. Too bad." He tut tutted with malicious glee. "A terrible man, your father, treating innocent foreigners like that? Oh, she would have paid all right to keep her precious Alex out of jail.

"It would have worked too, if he hadn't found out people were being cheated. But, fortune shines on the deserving and before he could tell anyone he ran into Anasta Thropyleus who wanted revenge for his brother's family being denied their insurance. Thropyleus knew you and your mother were in the house when he set it on fire and he waited for your father to arrive so he could tell him and then shoot him.

"But, your father grabbed the gun and in the struggle Thropyleus ended up shooting himself. Then afraid he would be tried for murder, your father panicked and ran. As I said, he was not too bright."

Cate's arm ached from Meyer's grip. She was afraid if she struggled he would kill her right then but thought, If I can keep him talking someone will come along and help me.

"Why are there three graves and who is buried in them?" she asked.

"Susannah, my sister, your mother, is buried there. And Thropyleus. We put him in Alex's box and yours was just rocks in a blanket."

"But why?"

Fredrick sighed heavily. "You are as slow as your father. For the money, of course. Susannah was dead and Thropyleus was dead. Susannah was lying on the ground at the foot of the ladder and Thropyleus was in the driveway. I dragged him into the house and by the time it burned down you couldn't tell who he was. I was pretty sure that Alex had run and even though Thropyleus was way too big to be Alex the firemen didn't pay much attention to the body so I sent for the undertaker who owed me money and told him to say that it was Alex. He didn't much like doing it but he would have liked me calling his loan a whole lot less.

"By burying him as your father I tidied up all the loose ends and avoided so many unpleasant questions. And, with both of you dead and buried, Susannah's money came to me." Frederick's voice hardened and swelled with anger. "Should have been mine anyway. Just because she had a clubfoot was no reason for our parents to leave her all of their money. Well, now it is mine. Mine and Nate's and no risen-from-the-grave niece is going to take it away!"

"I don't want the money," Cate spoke urgently, desperately. "I've never wanted the money. It's yours. It's Nate's. I don't want it."

"No?" sneered Frederic, "Then just why are you here poking your nose everywhere? Why are you asking questions about The German Slovenian Bank; looking up newspaper articles; hunting down old servants? Why?"

"I just ..." Cate started to say she just wanted to know who she was but feared he would think that meant to get the money. "I just wanted to know what happened to my father. I'm not interested in changing my name or getting any money. I can earn my own money. I just wanted to know about my father." Her voice trailed away.

The buggy moved out of the woods into the bright afternoon sunlight. Cate sat up looking eagerly ahead. The road stretched empty in front of them. In desperation she turned to God. Please help me, she prayed. Dear Lord, please send someone to help me.

Suddenly Meyer turned the buggy onto a rough trail that veered south away from the road. The buggy lurched down onto the old trail throwing Cate to the right and slamming her knee into the metal whip holder. Meyer's firm grip kept her from falling out of the buggy. Peggy did not like the new trail but Meyer also kept her firmly in hand. The horse obeyed but moved forward with ears laid back.

"Well, it's a good thing you do not want to change your name," Meyer said, "because it's not going to happen. No one but you and me will ever know you are my niece."

"Good. That's fine with me. I prefer it that way too." Cate tried to smile at Fredrick Meyer but he went on as if she had not spoken.

"Your father was a fool, too, when he came back to Red Jacket but at least he didn't lie to me."

"My father came back to Red Jacket?"

Meyer shook his head in disgust at Cate's stupidity. "How in the world do you think I found out about him knowing about the fraud and how the fire started and the name of the man who tried to kill him?

"So, yes. He came back. First day after he ran away he realized that he had made a big mistake. He decided to find a home for you and then return to Red Jacket to tell the truth.

He changed your name, too, so you wouldn't be put in an orphanage if no one believed him and he went to jail."

"Did they believe him?" Cate asked, casting about in her mind for an idea, a plan. Something, I've got to do something. I can't just let him kill me.

Meyer laughed, "They might have if the fool had gone to them first. But he was sure there'd be a warrant out for his arrest so he came back secretly, riding a horse, sleeping in the woods. He wanted to see me before anyone else. He said together we could find out who committed the fraud and then, the police would see he had no reason, other than self-defense, to kill Thropyleus.

"My, my he didn't much like it when I laughed at him and told him he was the biggest fool this side of Timbuktu. When I told him I'd been pulling that scam for years he was shocked. Here, he had thought I was such an upstanding citizen and kind brother-in-law. And why, he wanted to know, had I promoted him if I thought he was such a fool.

"Why? Well, that was obvious, because he was a good, earnest, honest fellow, so eager to please and make his way in the world. Gave the business a good image he did. And, because he always wanted to see the best in people, that is just what he did see. In other words, he was the perfect dupe.

"Marrying my sister wasn't part of the plan. When my parents died I convinced her to come and keep house for me. I knew sooner or later I'd wear her down and make her give me the management of her money. But she fell in love with your father and there was nothing I could do about it. One minute I was looking at getting my hands on a fortune and the next she's married and pregnant with you and then there were three people between me and the money.

"That's when I decided to set him up for the fraud. I knew I had to have an ace in the hole in case I got into a jam. When I told him that, he did not want to believe me.

'Fred!' he asks, finally starting to get angry. 'All these years I thought of you as an honest man, a man who promoted me and encouraged me because you saw value in my work. Was it all lies?'

"So I told him the truth. He was good accountant. He could have been a good banker but he was a babe in the woods when it came to crooks. I admitted I had liked him, until he married my sister.

"Ho boy! Did that get him." Frederick laughed again.

'Until, I married Susannah? But, but we thought you were pleased when we married?' he stammered.

"Well, of course you thought that." I told him. "You may be stupid, but I'm not. I knew that if you thought I didn't like the marriage you might move away and take the money with you."

Where were they going Cate worried as the buggy bounced over the rough ground? All she could see ahead were meadows and sky.

"Oh, my he was upset. Said he was going to march right down to the police and tell them all about his big, bad brother-in-law.

"I told him it was a too late for that. Meddling fool. He gotten away with a nice stash of money, enough to start a new life. Did he take advantage of it. No, not him. Not mister straight-and-narrow, do the-right-thing, raised in an orphanage, go to church, McLaren.

"He had to come back and try to ruin my life.!" Meyer spit out the words. "And now his whelp is trying to do the same thing. Trying to ruin my life. Mine and my son's.

"You wanted to know what happened to your father when he tried to ruin my life? I'll tell you. I killed him and put him in the old Johnson Mine. That's where he is, and that is where you are going to be."

The buggy reached the edge of the rolling meadows and the trail plunged downward. Cate's stomach lurched as they dropped over the edge and her heart sank when she saw the steep rocky trail winding down the mile-long hill. Peggy didn't like it either. She whinnied, stumbling and shying.

"I don't want the money," Cate repeated desperately. "I don't."

"Too late," said Meyer. "You McLarens are always too late."

Watching Meyer struggle to control the horse Cate wondered how he planned to kill her. He's not going to get away with this one so easy, she decided looking at the whip in its holder. Not if I can help it.

Grabbing the whip Cate snapped it at Peggy. The horse leaped forward and the buggy bounced.

"Stop that!" yelled Meyer, releasing his grip on Cate to control the horse.

Cate whacked the whip again. The buggy was careening down the steep hill totally out of control as Cate leaped out.

Meyer, yelling and cursing, tried to control the horse but the buggy hit a boulder, bounced, bounced again, then flipped over and began tumbling downhill.

Cate hit the ground, hard. Her face plowed into the dirt, then her momentum carried her forward and she tumbled head over heels downhill until slamming up against a large rock.

Jamie arrived early for their meeting, so eager to tell Cate his news that he could not wait until four o'clock. But, it was Mrs. Sincock who opened the door and dashed his hopes saying, "I'm sorry, Mr. Dunn, but Cate took the buggy for ride in the country."

"Alone?" he asked, hoping he did not show how alarmed he felt.

"Yes, I believe so. She hasn't been gone very long. Was she expecting you?" Anna asked.

"Not until 4 o'clock," Jamie admitted.

"Well, I'm sure she will be here then," Anna reassured him.

"Yes. Of course. And thank you. I'll be back then."

Jamie hurried back to the lumber yard. I can't believe she went off by herself, he thought. And what will she do if the horse gets frightened and rears or gallops!

By the time Jamie was saddled and mounted he decided Cate would go where she had been before, where she had her lesson. A fast trot through town changed to a full gallop past the mines out on to the countryside.

Constantly scanning the road ahead Jamie was disappointed not to see Cate coming towards him. He slowed to an easy canter when the road entered the forest and soon arrived at the small meadow. She was not there. No one was there.

Then where? Surely she wouldn't have gone past the meadow. Would she? Unless, she couldn't turn the horse into the meadow? Puzzled, he thought, maybe that's what happened, she kept going because she had to.

Jamie followed the road through the forest and across the treeless plain until he reached the spot where the road began its long curving path downward. Looking down he saw a lumber wagon crossing the road at the bottom and two men on horseback. There were no buggies in sight.

Slowly he turned and began to canter back. She must have taken another road, he decided. If she was on this one and had a problem I would have seen some sign of it. He tried to reassure himself but fear itched. Something was wrong and he rode along looking carefully to the left and to the right. Nearing the forest he saw fresh tracks leading from the road onto an old trail and horse droppings that looked recent.

He dismounted to examine the droppings. They were fresh and the tracks could have been from a buggy. He followed the tracks on the old trail.

Jamie wasn't familiar with this fading old trail. It could barely be called a trail and it didn't make sense for Cate to be on it. He told himself he was wasting his time but fresh tire tracks pulled him along. He reached the edge of the plateau thinking, I'll look down the hill and see this trail will be as empty as the road.

At first it did seem that way. Then his eyes found the mangled mess of wagon and horses. Stunned, Jamie stared. Was Cate there? He tied his horse to a rough bush and ran, sliding and slipping on the steep, rocky path.

Two dead horses were tangled with the destroyed buggy and a man lay trapped in the wreckage. Carefully, Jamie edged around the shattered wreck wondering who he was and if he was alive. He was startled to see Fredrick

Meyer and he was most definitely dead. Looking at the horses again, Jamie realized Sincock's horse had been pulling the buggy.

WHERE WAS CATE? She had to be here. He looked frantically around searching the nearby bushes. If not here, where? Think! Could she have jumped? Heart pounding with exertion and panic, he ran to the top of the hill and began looking again.

There! Down the hill to the right, against that boulder.

Dear Lord, Please let her be all right, he prayed running to Cate. Jammed against the rock she lay face down, unmoving. Carefully, Jamie rolled her over. Gently he touched her battered and bleeding face. "Cate," he said. She did not reply but lay unconscious, breathing so lightly he could barely detect it. But she was breathing. She was alive. Alive!

Carefully placing one arm under her knees and the other supporting her back and head he picked her up and turned to face the hill.

Chapter 15

Cate drifted towards the light. The light came near. And sound was there, too. Sound and light. She opened her eyes and saw a white wall and a window with sunlight pouring in. She began to turn her head but stabbing pain and nausea made her lie still. Very slowly she tried again to turn her head and this time succeeded. Mrs. Ogilve sat in a chair by her bed, reading. Cate closed her eyes and slept.

When she woke up again Mrs. Ogilve was looking at her. "Catherine, are you awake?"

"Yes," Cate whispered, her throat dry and raspy. Then to her astonishment she burst into tears as she reached out to the woman who had become her mother.

Tears also ran down Mrs. Ogilve's face as she hugged Cate.

"You gave us a fright, young lady," said Dr. Bear who was standing at the foot of her bed. "You have been unconscious for five days. How do you feel?"

"Tired. I'm tired," said Cate.

"Yes. Well, that's to be expected," he said, then smiled as Cate fell back asleep. "She will be all right now," he assured Mrs. Ogilve. "As far as we can tell there are no broken bones, though I expect she may have fractured some ribs. We'll know that when she begins to move about. The real worries were the head injuries but now that she has finally come out of the coma and recognized you I expect she will make a full recovery."

Cate left the hospital three days later walking very carefully fearing a careless movement that brought sharp, piercing pain to her fractured ribs. She was eager to escape the constant attention of the hospital staff along with everyone waiting for her to remember and tell them about the accident.

Dr. Bear had been kind and helpful assuring Cate that it was not at all unusual for someone who had a concussion to be unable to remember how it happened. But, he assured her, most people eventually remember. She was not to worry and dwell on it, it would come in its own time. And he told the sheriff not to bother her, that Cate would come to them when she remembered. The sheriff agreed saying, "After all, it was not as if we were dealing with a crime, everyone knew it was an accident."

Cate was grateful for Dr. Bear's help and advice. She had been confused with no memory of how she came to be in the hospital the day she regained consciousness. But that following evening a student nurse gave Cate a sponge bath and said, "Oh, Miss. I'm so happy you woke up and didn't die from that terrible, terrible accident that killed Mr. Meyer. It is a miracle you are alive. Yes, it is. The doctor said it was Mr. Dunn finding you that saved your life."

And then Cate remembered. Remembered the fear that almost paralyzed her as the buggy bounced on and on with Fredrick Meyer speaking of killing her with as much concern in his voice as if she were a chicken. But he was dead. Did I kill him? she wondered as the images of the whip in her hand, beating down upon Peggy flashed through her mind.

She felt sick as she pictured the horse tumbling down the steep hill. Poor beast did not deserve to die like that. Troubled and sick at heart she fell asleep wondering what she should, what she could, say about that day.

John Sincock drove Cate home from the hospital in a handsome new buggy pulled by a high-stepping black gelding. Cate wondered how much they cost. She determined to find out and repay them. Mrs. Sincock was waiting on the front porch, eager to fuss over Cate, making her feel welcome and cherished.

"Now, you sit right out here on the porch," she commanded. "It's much cooler than inside and I'll bring out lunch right out here."

How beautiful everything looks, Cate thought. Butterflies darted among the flowers lining the front walk and two robins were busy flying to and from their nest in the maple tree shading the porch. A feeling of joy welled up in Cate as she silently prayed, "Dear Lord, thank you for this beautiful world. And thank you for my safe delivery from Fredrick Meyer. Please Lord, tell me what to do now. I keep thinking of Nate, I see him coming home from fishing, so happy and proud of his father. Now, he must live with the pain of his father's death. Do I destroy the pride and love he feels too? If I tell the truth, who will it help? Lord, I don't know what to do."

"Here we are!" Mrs. Sincock said coming through the door. Startled, Cate jumped, then sucked in her breath as her fractured ribs gripped. "I have chicken sandwiches and lemonade right here. Mr. Sincock had to go back to work and Mrs. Ogilve won't be here till supper time so it just you and me. Now, you sit right here while I go in and get the salad and cookies."

Cate smiled. It was good to be home.

After dinner that evening the Sincocks and Mrs. Ogilve attended church. Cate was instructed to stay home and rest. She settled down in the parlor to read the August edition of The Music Teacher's magazine. The doorbell interrupted before she reached the end of the first article.

"Jamie!" Cate's heart seemed to skip a beat when she opened the door and saw Jamie standing there. A delighted smile spread across his face at her enthusiastic welcome.

"Come in, come in. I'm so glad you're here, there is so much I want to tell you and to ask you." Placing his straw hat on the hall table Jamie followed Cate into the parlor.

Watching how carefully she walked and how tentatively she took her seat, he asked, "Are you sure you want a visitor? Shouldn't you be resting?"

"I've been resting for days. I'm so rested I'd even begun to wonder why you didn't come to see me," Cate said, tipping her head sideways, looking at him half teasing, half serious.

"I did go to the hospital every day when you were unconscious," Jamie hurried to assure her. "But, once you woke up and the doctor said you were going to be fine I was able to go with Mr. Charbonneau to the livery and carriage merchants convention in Detroit. I just returned this morning."

"A livery and carriage convention?" Cate was puzzled.

"Yes." Jamie nodded and took a deep breath. "You know I came to this country because I wanted to own my own business. When Mr. Charbonneau hired me to work for him, he asked me what my ambitions were and I told him. He watched my work and encouraged from the beginning, even taking me into the office sometimes to learn about ledgers and accounting.

"Then, three weeks ago he told me Herman Baumgarten's hauling and livery business was for sale. They deliver most of the logs we buy from the logging companies and Mr. Charbonneau was concerned that a new owner might not want to haul logs. He said he would buy the company if I would run it."

"Jamie, that's wonderful."

"That's not all," said Jamie, "he wants me to buy the business from him. When I asked him why he would do that he said one business was enough to run." Astonishment over his good fortune was clear in his voice.

Cate was thrilled for Jamie. "This is wonderful. Mr. Charbonneau must be a very special man."

"He is," Jamie affirmed. "You'll see when you meet him. And I found out I'm not the only person he has done this for. Donald MacDonald told me Mr. Charbonneau financed his grocery store in Laurium and Eric Barkel's furniture store in Hancock."

"This is the plan." He leaned forward in his chair, eager to tell Cate everything. "I will be paid a salary. Of course I'll save from the salary but it won't be enough, by itself, to buy the business. But Mr. Charbonneau has set it up so that at the end of the year we will divide the profits. My half will go to pay back Mr. C's original investment. Once he has received all of his investment, the company will be mine. And that is fair as far as I can see because he is putting up all of the money and taking the risk that I'll be able to make enough money to pay him."

Cate smiled and shook her head in wonder. "That is just amazing. And wonderful."

"It is," a beaming Jamie agreed. Then he became serious. "We signed the agreement two Saturdays ago. As soon as it was done I came to tell you. I just couldn't wait until our 4 o'clock appointment.

"But you weren't here! I was worried about you driving alone with so little experience and went to find you."

"That's why you found me before the thunderstorm."

"Yes. And I when I saw you lying there my heart stopped. I could not breathe until I finally felt your heartbeat."

"Did you?" Cate looked away. "Did you see Meyer, too?"

"Yes, I saw him first."

"And the horses," she whispered. "Were they alive?"

"No."

With a large sigh Cate eased back in her chair. "Thank you. It's bothered me so much. Thinking that Peggy suffered and the other horse, too, but I knew Peggy and she was a good horse. I hated to think of her suffering."

"You do remember what happened?" Jamie asked. "I'd heard you didn't remember that day."

"Well, Dr. Bear said I might not and when I very first woke up I didn't and then when I did, I didn't know what to say."

"And now?"

"Now I want to tell you what happened." Cate began haltingly, trying to remember everything. Jamie listened intently with no interruptions as he could see it was not easy for Cate to speak of that day.

There was silence when she finished. Then Jamie said, "You used the whip. That was good thinking. Very good thinking. I'm proud of you."

"Proud of me?" Cate was astonished.

"Yes."

"But, I killed a man."

"You were just protecting yourself," Jamie asserted firmly.

"But will others think that? Or will they refuse to send their children to Miss Duncan's music class because I killed a man?"

"That could happen," Jamie agreed reluctantly. "But do they need to know?"

"I've been struggling with that and I've decided they do not need to know. I can say it was an accident. That the horses panicked and I don't remember anything after that.

"I know that is not telling the truth but Fredrick Meyer ruined enough of my life. Here, it stops. He is not going to prevent me from teaching and get me thrown in jail for murder." Cate would have pounded her fist on the arm of her chair if her ribs would have permitted it.

"I'm not sure yet what I'm going to remember from the rest of the day. I've no desire to hurt Nate but there is the matter of my father lying in the mine. I want to find him and bury him where he belongs, next to my mother."

"Did Meyer tell you where in the mine he was buried."

"No. I don't think so. He just said he killed him there and left him there."

"My brother, Donald, and I will look. The Johnson Mine is different from the Hecla mines. They have shafts going straight down into the earth and you need a mechanical lift to get up and down. The Johnson Mine goes sideways into the hill and one walks in. I'm not a miner but my brother is and the two of us could go and see what we can find."

Jamie promised to begin the search the following evening and Cate, exhausted emotionally and physically, was asleep before the Sincocks returned from church.

Friday morning a young boy from the Livery Stable delivered a letter to Cate.

Thursday, Aug., 28

Dear Cate,

We have just returned from the Johnson Mine. It is too late to call at the Sincocks so I undertake to write this now that you may know the results of our search first thing tomorrow.

We entered the Johnson Mine but the tunnels are blocked from numerous cave-ins. Donald says they were not braced correctly and now are collapsing. Where we were able to search we carefully examined the ground but did not find anything.

> *I am so sorry we could not be more helpful.*
> *Sincerely,*
> *Jamie*

Gently Cate placed the letter with her father's papers then picked up the family photograph and examined her father's face. All these years I've been so angry with you and you weren't even alive, she thought. I just wanted you to come back and I didn't understand why you didn't. Now, I do. You must have been a good man to have tried to stop the fraud.

Cate's eyes overflowed with tears as she thought about her father. When the tears stopped, Cate wiped her eyes and blew her nose. Now, she knew what she wanted to do. She would write to Florence Meyer requesting a meeting at three o'clock that afternoon at Sincocks when they would be undisturbed because it was Freda's day off and Mrs. Sincock and Mrs. Ogilve would be taking tea with Mrs. Anderson.

Mrs. Meyer agreed to the meeting.

Cate prepared carefully for Mrs. Meyer's arrival. Over her summer corset she wore a soft, light blue, cotton dress decorated with dark blue silk at the wrists and waist. She brushed her hair until it shone, then tied it with a dark blue ribbon letting the curls fall naturally.

She sighed looking at her face. There wasn't anything she could do about the black eye tinged with yellow, the scabs and new pink skin covering scrapes on her chin and nose, nor the bandage over the gash on her forehead.

The doorbell rang at three. When Cate opened the door, Florence Meyer walked past her not even bothering to glance at her and proceeded to the parlor. She sat down and removed her lace gloves.

Cate felt her heart pounding and annoyed with herself and attempting to calm down walked slowly to the parlor and sat down. She waited until Florence Meyer finally looked at her and then spoke.

"I asked you to meet with me today because I must decide what I am going to say about the day that Mr. Meyer died."

Florence looked keenly interested but remained silent.

Cate plunged on. "I do not know if Mr. Meyer told you he was my uncle?" From the widening of Florence's eyes Cate was sure he had not. "But, he was, and I can prove it, if that is necessary."

Cate paused, but Florence Meyer retained her composure and her silence.

"In June I came to Red Jacket looking for answers about my father, who disappeared when I was five-years old. And for the truth about myself because of documents we found that indicated I was Catherine McLaren, not Catherine Duncan.

In the Red Jacket cemetery I discovered three tombstones, my father's, Alexander Duncan McLaren, mine, Catherine Alexandra McLaren and my mother's, Susannah Meyer McLaren. I had been told she died in a fire and searching from the date on the tombstone I found an article in the newspaper about the fire that destroyed the McLaren family. It also mentioned that Frederick Meyer was the brother of Susannah Meyer McLaren, and business associate of Alexander McLaren.

"Among my father's papers there was also evidence of insurance fraud committed when Mr. Meyer ran the German Slovenian Miners Bank. He sold insurance to miners whose relatives lived in Europe and when that miner died the insurance company paid but Mr. Meyer did not send it to the family, he kept it for himself and told the family the insurance had lapsed.

"Mr. Meyer discovered I was asking questions and began to investigate me. When he realized we were related he assumed I was after the money from my mother's estate. I wasn't, but he didn't believe it.

"On the day he died I went for a ride in the buggy by myself. He followed me, found me picking wildflowers, forced me onto the buggy and drove towards the Johnson mine. He told me that he knew I was his niece, that no one was in my grave, and a foreigner was buried as my father. He had done that because then he was the only heir to my mother's money. He said my father came back looking for help and told him that he had run away because he had killed the man that set fire to our house and was afraid he would go to jail and I would be put in an orphanage. To prevent that he had hidden me under a different name so I would be raised in a good home if anything happened to him. My father came to his brother-in-law for help and was murdered instead. Killed and left in the abandoned Johnson mine because Fredrick Meyer was determined to keep his sister's fortune.

"On that terrible ride he mocked the people he'd cheated and said I was as big a fool as my father to get upset over foreigners. And he was going to do the same thing to me that he did to my father, kill me and leave me in the mine. I told him over and over that I did not want my mother's money! He didn't believe me.

"But, I believed him! When the horse shied going over the edge of the steep hill I grabbed the whip, whipped the horse, and leaped from the carriage."

Florence continued to sit erectly, listen and remain silent.

Cate took a deep breath and continued. "Now, I must decide what to tell the sheriff. If by remaining silent about much of what happened that day I can ensure that the people who were cheated out of their insurance money get paid I am willing to do it. I cannot change the past and most of what has happened, but this one thing, I can correct. It will be one thing Frederick Meyer will not get away with!" Cate said, anger surging through her voice. "The people will get their money."

Finally, Florence spoke, "Including you?"

"No. Not including me. I do not want money. Nor do I plan to take back the McLaren name. I will remain Catherine Duncan."

"You have proof of this fraud?" Florence asked.

"Yes. I have 70 letters that have been translated by Rev. Heimonen, Father Pawler and Father Karinen. Would you like me to get them?"

Florence thought for a moment. "No. How much money are you talking about?"

"Thirty thousand dollars. One thousand for each policy.'

"You said 70 letters?"

"They are letters looking for payment and letters explaining why payment was denied and some people wrote more than once but there are only thirty addresses."

"Thirty thousand." Florence thought about the amount. "Yes, that could be done but only if it is keep confidential. What assurance do I have of that?"

"The translation of the letters was undertaken on a strictly confidential basis. I'm sure if they understand the payments are connected to maintaining that commitment, they will honor it."

"Let us hope so," Florence stated. "For if the matter becomes public all payments will stop. If I agree to this, what will you say happened that day?"

"I will say that I have remembered that I was picking wildflowers when Mr. Meyer came along. He stopped to say hello and water his horse. While we talked he said he was on his way to the old Johnson Mine and suggested I might like to come along because it was a rare chance for a female to go into a mine. That he told me miners do not let women in mines because they bring bad luck. But the Johnson mine was abandoned so this was a once in a lifetime opportunity. I will say that we were talking about music and not paying proper attention when we suddenly dropped over the ridge, the horse panicked and bolted and I was tossed out of the carriage."

Florence looked at Cate, studying her carefully. Finally, she asked, "Why? Why are you willing to do this?"

"Because of Nate. I keep seeing him coming home after fishing with his father. How excited and happy he was. Or the night of the musical, looking over at his father with such love in his eyes. Now that father is gone, all Nate has are his memories. If I tell what happened, I will destroy those memories. I remember what it was like to lose a father and to lose the love and trust I'd had in him. I don't want to do that to Nate if I can, in good conscience, avoid it.

"I've struggled with telling what happened. If Mr. Meyer were alive it would not be a question. If my father were alive it would not be a question. I cannot punish the one or restore the other. Correcting the insurance fraud is the closest I can come to either."

Florence nodded slowly, accepting Cate's explanation. "All right. You speak to the authorities and if your story is accepted I will have my lawyer set up a fund for thirty thousand dollars. The religious men can write the letters and make the payments. One hundred dollars will be given each man to compensate him for his time and, a five hundred dollar contribution to each church if confidentiality is maintained in this matter.

"Also, you are never to mention the Meyer name in relation to this fund. It comes from an anonymous citizen. I must have your word on that."

"You have it."

Florence picked up her gloves and began drawing them on. "It is settled then; we are agreed. You will speak to the authorities and tell them that Frederick died in a tragic accident. I will make arrangements for the thirty thousand dollar fund."

"Yes," Cate affirmed.

Florence stood and stared down at Cate. "I'm still puzzled that you are doing this and I hope it truly is because you care for Nate. And not because you need time to gather evidence of your relationship to Fredrick's sister planning to contest her estate in the future. Because," she stepped closer, her eyes and voiced hardening, "I want you to understand one thing, if you are playing with me, if you do not adhere to your word, to your every word, then, I will make it my life's work to destroy you—and I will succeed!"

Florence turned and swept out of the room. Exhausted, Cate sat unmoving wondering if she had won or lost.

That evening Jamie, Mrs. Ogilve and Cate sat on the side porch. It had been awkward telling Mrs. Sincock that she wished to speak with Mrs. Ogilve privately but she had taken it in good grace.

Cate told Mrs. Ogilve everything that had happened starting with the drunk attacking her at night. It was a long conversation with Mrs. Ogilve asking many questions. Cate was anxious for her reaction to her decision not to tell the sheriff what really happened.

"This is a most unusual situation," said Mrs. Ogilve. "In this situation, Catherine, I'm afraid telling the truth might be the worst thing you could do. Why? Because, while you, Mr. Dunn and I know that what you told us really happened, not everyone will believe you. After all, it is only your word against the reputation of a wealthy and prominent member of the community.

"And there is no way to prove the attacks upon you. For instance, the man who attacked you at night. Nobody saw that. And even if they did it is only your word that Fredrick Meyer ordered it. You could be making it up.

"And the melody you remember from your childhood. You say it is the same as Susannah Meyer's composition but again how could you prove it?

"Even your father's murder. We cannot search the mine where he was killed to prove that part of the story and there is a body buried under his name in the cemetery. You see the problem?"

"You are right," Jamie agreed. "Even with the fraud we found. The translators say the letters have different signatures but they all say Alexander McLaren. Instead of proving Meyer committed fraud it might end up just the way he planned with the blame falling on your father.

"You told me yesterday you were struggling with the fact that the truth would not help you and it would hurt Nate. Now I think adding what Mrs. Ogilve has pointed out, that the truth would most likely cause great hurt to you also ... well, given that, I think you have done exactly the right thing. Don't you agree Mrs. Ogilve?"

"Yes. I certainly do."

"I'm so glad you both think I did the right thing. I'd already cast my lot by speaking with Florence Meyer but knowing that you support my decision is a great relief."

"When will you talk to the sheriff?" Jamie asked.

"I'd like to get that over with as soon as possible. Tomorrow morning if he'll see me."

"He'll see you," Jamie assured her. "Let him know you will go to his office at eleven. I'll pick you up at 10:30 and go with you."

The following morning, Cate was surprised how easily it all went. The sheriff treated her with great kindness, took her statement, congratulated her on her survival and sent her on her way. They were soon back at Sincocks.

"Can you stay for lunch?" Cate asked as Jamie her helped from the buggy.

"I wish I could. But I have an appointment with Mr. Baumgarten to go over the business accounts. I'm trying to learn as much from him as I can while he's here. His wife has always wanted to travel and now that he has sold the business she is ready to go. He is trying to delay leaving for awhile because there is so much I need to know but she is getting impatient. So I don't want to keep him waiting. Besides, I'll be coming to dinner Tuesday evening." He laughed seeing Cate's surprise.

"To the Sincocks farewell dinner party for Mrs. Ogilve? Oh, Jamie I'm so glad. I ... I'm just so glad."

"I'm not so sure I am," Jamie confessed.

"Why not?" Cate was alarmed.

"I've never been to dinner party. I'm not sure how to dress or even the proper way to act."

"Ah," Cate smiled. "Well, you taught me to drive a buggy. I can teach you about dinner parties."

"I'd like that," Jamie said, opening the Sincock's front door for Cate.

"So would I," she responded softly. They stood looking into each other's eyes.

Taking a deep breath, Jamie backed away a step, smiled, turned and hurried down the porch steps. When he reached the buggy, he turned around and saw Cate still standing in the doorway, looking at him. Joyfully, he half bowed and tipped his hat. Smiling, he drove off.

Cate smiled too. Yes, she decided, this is going to be a wonderful year.

The End.

Made in the USA
Middletown, DE
08 July 2023